BLUE MOON

BLUE MOON

PATRICIA H. SQUIRE

The Book Guild Ltd

First published in Great Britain in 2023 by
The Book Guild Ltd
Unit E2 Airfield Business Park,
Harrison Road, Market Harborough,
Leicestershire. LE16 7UL
Tel: 0116 2792299
www.bookguild.co.uk
Email: info@bookguild.co.uk
Twitter: @bookguild

This work is entirely fictitious and bears no resemblance to any persons living or dead.

Typeset in 11pt Minion Pro

Printed and bound in the UK by TJ Books LTD, Padstow, Cornwall

ISBN 978 1915352 606

British Library Cataloguing in Publication Data.
A catalogue record for this book is available from the British Library.

For my grandson Alexander Squire, I hope you enjoy this tale one day.

Also, as always, for David for his unfailing encouragement.

CHAPTER ONE

Esme heard the key in the front door. 'Good timing,' she called out. 'I'm just serving up supper.'

Matt came into the kitchen and enthusiastically kissed her before taking his seat at the table. He was still getting used to coming home to a tidy flat and supper prepared for him. They had gone through a couple of sticky patches and he would never again take her for granted. She was the sparkling centre of his universe.

Once the meal was dished out and they began to eat, Matt asked, 'So how was your day. You were over at the Blue Moon, weren't you?'

'Oh, Matt, it was so sad. Enid Hopjoy died last night.'

He eyed her quizzically. 'It is an old people's home, love. Bound to have the inmates die off fairly regularly.'

She put her knife and fork down and looked at him reproachfully. 'First, it's a select home for those in their twilight years, not "an old people's home", and second, Enid was lovely. She was quite quiet and unassuming. Then she'd say something shocking and you'd stare at her in surprise until you saw the twinkle in her eye.' Esme heaved a great sigh. 'She was really liked by the staff as well as the other residents. She will be greatly missed.' Esme fell into a reverie.

'Esme.' Matt brought her back to the present. 'Come on, love. Eat your supper. And I'm sorry about her death. I can see it's upset you.'

Esme nodded and resumed her meal.

'What I don't understand,' Matt said, 'is how you get so involved with the residents. You're only there two or three mornings a week to keep their accounts in order. I don't see how you get to know them.'

Matt and Esme had met while she worked for an import/export company that had collapsed after various smuggling activities came to light. Matt had been the investigating police officer. Instead of looking for a new position, Esme had decided to fast-track her career goals and start up as a freelance bookkeeper. Blue Moon had been her first client and she had a soft spot for them. Felicia Rogers, who had known Esme from their previous employment, had secured a position as secretary to Blue Moon's owner after Holtexim folded. She had recommended Esme as a bookkeeper – possibly motivated by seeking to make amends after trying to implicate Esme in the illegal activities at their former place of work.

'They're not that many of them, only twelve when full, and it's inevitable we got to know each other. Sometimes they might wander into the office with a query or maybe just looking for a chat. Also, I usually spend my break with some of them and, of course, I join them for lunch in the dining room. So, you see, it would be hard not to get to know them.'

Matt smiled. 'It's you, Esme. People like you, they gravitate to you and the reason is that you like them. You are genuinely interested in them and that's a great draw.'

'Oh posh.' Esme stood to clear their plates, but she flushed slightly, pleased he thought of her that way. 'Do you want cheese or ice cream?'

After due consideration, Matt selected cheese and she bustled round, producing a small board with a selection of cheeses and a basket of biscuits. They made their choices and began to eat.

'I just hope,' Esme said, 'that the new resident is as nice as Enid and will fit in with the others.'

'The residents won't be unwelcoming, will they? Resent the newcomer just because they're replacing someone they liked?'

'Oh no, I'm sure not. The thing is, they're sort of in groups.'

'Groups?'

'Yes. Nothing organised, just those with similar interests naturally tend to mix together.'

'Cliques, you mean. If so, that will pose a problem for the newcomer. Cliques are notorious for being reluctant to allow anyone new within their circles.'

'No. Not cliques. These aren't closed groups. They all mix together but, for instance, take Jane, Penny, Larry and Bob. They all like doing crosswords – from the Daily Telegraph, of course.'

'Of course,' Matt murmured.

Ignoring him, Esme continued, 'They play Mah Jong, like listening to current-affairs programmes on the radio and enjoy similar tastes in films – particularly musicals. So, naturally, they spend a lot of time together pursuing their common interests. Oh, and I mustn't forget lime marmalade.'

'Lime marmalade?'

'Yes. Everyone else has orange marmalade or jam. But

the four of them have to sit at the same breakfast table as they all prefer lime marmalade.'

'I see.' A short silence ensued until Matt asked, 'So, who did Enid spend most of her time with?'

'Enid was more of a floater. She liked musicals too, so would join Jane, Penny and co to watch them. If she wanted to go shopping, quite often Lucy or Celia, or both, would accompany her. However, on the whole, I suppose she was most often with Alice.'

'Alice. I've heard of her before.'

'Yes, because she is the Chair of the Residents' Association. A sort of conduit for any problems between residents and management or staff. They also organise trips and entertainments. I probably mention her the most as she comes to the office to sort things out or arrange their events.'

'I see.' Matt rose and started to clear the table. 'Still,' he added mischievously, 'I'm not sure I see much difference between your established groups and cliques.'

Esme laughed and retrieved a towel to dry the dishes as Matt washed them. The conversation switched to Matt's day. Esme enjoyed hearing about Rick Preston, Matt's partner. He could be a bit brash and sometimes came up with the most off-the-wall comments or actions. That made her laugh. However, Matt liked him and thought he was shaping up to be a good officer.

ॐॐ

Meanwhile, across town, the Carstairs family were also discussing the death of Enid Hopjoy while they ate their supper. Neil Carstairs was the owner and director of Blue Moon. Following a stress-induced collapse while pursuing his financial career, he had decided to downsize his work responsibilities by buying and running Blue Moon. He and his family, comprising himself, his wife Paula and nineteen-year-old daughter Selina, lived in an annexe to the main building.

'I just hope the new resident will fit in easily with the others,' Neil said.

'Yes,' Paula agreed. 'I'm sorry about Enid. We often had little chats which I really enjoyed. She sometimes had a unique way of looking at things which seemed to make problems so much clearer to deal with. And the rest of the guests all liked her, which was quite an achievement, given how different some are. It could be difficult for her replacement to fill her shoes, I suppose.'

'I wouldn't worry,' Selina broke in. 'Whoever it is will just latch on to one the "sets" and soon no one will even remember Enid clearly.'

'Selina!' Paula was appalled. 'What a wicked thing to say, or even think.'

Selina shrugged.

Neil frowned at his daughter. 'A bit more respect would be nice for both Enid and your mother.'

'Whatever.' Selina was not concerned. She had other bigger battles to fight.

After a short, frustrated pause, Neil turned to his wife. 'Enid's family, or at least a couple of them, are coming tomorrow. Would you mind supervising the packing up of all her belongings?'

'Of course. I'll speak to Sonja first thing in the morning.' Paula had few personal goals in life, but her main one was to look after her family. She had always been a natural worrier, but Neil's collapse had intensified this trait and she lived in fear of losing him. She was willing to do anything she could to lighten his pressures at work.

Selina cleared the table and began to rinse the crockery before stacking it in the dishwasher. Her mother meanwhile switched off the coffee percolator and started to fill cups.

'Do you want coffee this evening?' she asked Selina, who occasionally warned them about the dangers of caffeine to their health – despite having a part-time job in the village coffee shop.

'No thanks, Mum. I'm going out. No time.'

Neil, still sitting at the table glancing at the headlines in the paper, looked up. 'Where are you going?'

'Zoggo is having a practice session with his band. I've got to be there to provide support and help, if needed.'

'Zoggo!' Neil harrumphed. 'What sort of name is Zoggo, anyway?'

'Look, Dad, you don't like him, I do. You don't have to see him and I like to. I don't see what your problem is.'

'He eats enough meals here, so I do have to see him. My problem with him, apart from his name, is that he's a no-good layabout, whose music is cacophonous with no melody and, distressingly, sounds all the same.'

Selina slammed down a dish, causing her mother to wince. 'You just don't understand him. He's a true artist.' Neil snorted but she continued, undeterred. 'He gave up conventional living for the sake of his music.' She flounced out of the room.

Paula placed a cup in front of Neil and looked at him reproachfully.

'I know,' he said. 'I know. But I hate to see her wasting her time on such a bozo. She's much too good for him. I thought her too intelligent to believe all this "giving up conventional living for the sake of his music" crap.'

Paula sat opposite him with her own cup. 'She is

intelligent and I've no doubt she'll eventually come to see Zoggo with clear eyes one day.'

Neil grunted. 'Can't come too soon.' He looked at his wife, 'I blame this gap year before going to university. And,' he warmed to his theme, 'why is she so determined to study music? It's a hobby – unless you're truly exceptional, which she is not. She's good,' he hastily went on as Paula looked ready to defend her daughter, 'but she's never going to make a living at it, except maybe teaching a rotational crop of children who would rather be doing something – preferably anything – else!'

Paula sipped her coffee. 'It's her life, darling. You can't live it for her. You can only advise. In the end she has to make her own decisions.'

'Even though it's the wrong one?' But he was smiling, she saw with relief. His stress level had settled down.

'Yes,' she said firmly, and rose to finish loading the dishwasher.

CHAPTER TWO

Early on a Friday afternoon, Rose Johns arrived at Blue Moon. Neil, Paula and Sonja, the assistant director, came out onto the front steps as Rose's taxi swept up. Neil went down to open the taxi door for her.

'Welcome to Blue Moon,' he greeted her.

Rose accepted his hand to help her out, then stood looking around. Finally, she turned to Neil. 'My luggage is in the boot. No doubt the driver will help you – if he wants a tip, that is.'

She then climbed the steps where Paula and Sonja waited. Neil and the driver exchanged speaking glances then began to unload the car.

Paula, slightly unnerved at Rose's behaviour, left it to Sonja to lead her to the office where a few formalities needed attention. Following this, she said brightly, 'I'll take you to see your room now. Tea is at four o'clock, but you may wish to rest before meeting your fellow guests.'

'I'll see the room, but I'm not so frail as to need to take an afternoon nap.'

'Right. Good. Well, this way then.' Sonja led the way

while Paula cravenly remained in the office. The omens were not looking good.

Shortly, Sonja reappeared and sank in a chair. 'My God. What a woman.' She fixed Paula with her eyes. 'The room is smaller than she was led to believe. The décor needs refreshing. It has not been cleaned to her satisfaction, even though she had to inspect the back of the wardrobe floor to find a speck of dust for that complaint.' She sighed as she leant back. 'I left as soon as Neil and the driver appeared with her baggage. Cowardly, I know.'

'No, not at all. Perhaps it's just she's tired or nervous about settling in here.' Paula, ever the peacemaker who tried to find good in everyone, however hard!

Sonja cocked her head. 'That woman, nervous? I sincerely doubt it.'

'Oh dear. I hope she's not going to cause trouble.'

'I have no doubt she will. I took her upstairs, you can collect her for tea when the time comes.'

'Sounds fair.' Fair, but not at all what she wanted. Nevertheless, at the appointed time Paula accompanied Rose to the dining room. Naturally all eyes were on the newcomer, as Paula led Rose to the table where Alice and Peter sat.

'Rose, this is Alice Littleton and Peter Francis. Alice, Peter, this is our new guest, Rose Johns.'

The three nodded at each other and Alice said, 'Nice to meet you. Would you join us for tea?'

Rose thanked her and sat down.

Paula cleared her throat. 'Alice is the Chair of the Residents' Association. She and Peter, her deputy, basically act as liaison with management over any problems the residents may have as well as organising a variety of activities.'

'I see.' Rose looked at Alice closely. 'A useful person to know.'

Alice smiled uncertainly while Paula said, 'Good. I'll leave you to get to know each other over tea,' before making her escape.

Alice, with Peter's stalwart support, regaled a mostly silent Rose with information on their forthcoming planned outings and entertainments. After tea they introduced her to the others, who were all eager to meet her and try to make her feel welcome.

However, by suppertime the residents were well on the way to realising that Rose could not be less like Enid if she tried. She was the last person to enter the dining room for supper. As she looked round no one met her eyes and nearly everyone appeared to be engrossed in fascinating conversations. She sniffed and made her way to where Wally and Al sat. If they were not alone, these two could usually be found together. Both had enjoyed very successful high-flying careers, both were widowers and they understood each other.

'May I join you?' Rose rested a hand on the back of an empty chair.

'Of course.' Wally nodded.

Rose sat and examined the menu, printed on a card in the centre of the table. 'I see there's only a choice between two items,' she observed.

'Yes,' said Wally. Not one to waste his words.

After a pause, Al added, 'Two choices at every meal.'

Rose pursed her lips as Marjorie, or Marj, as she liked to be known, bustled up to take their orders. Wally smiled at her. 'I'll have the Welsh rarebit, please, Marj.'

Al inclined his head. 'I'll have the same, please.'

Marj jotted their choices onto a pad attached to string

hanging from her waist. She turned to Rose. 'And what can I get for you?'

'Neither particularly appeals, but I suppose it'll have to be the ham and mushroom omelette.'

Marj raised an eyebrow at the two men before noting it down then hurried on to the next table.

Rose looked at Wally and Al, who returned the gaze. 'How long have you been here?' she asked.

'Three years,' Al said.

'Just over two years,' Wally replied.

After a pause, Rose tried again. 'I met Alice at tea.'

'Yes,' Al finally acknowledged.

'I must say I can't imagine her successfully organising events. Not the type.'

'She doesn't do it alone,' Al answered.

'The Residents' Association is democratic. Alice chairs it – very well, in my opinion,' Wally added.

The meal arrived and was eaten in silence. After the pudding had been served Marj came to see if they wanted coffee.

'Might as well,' Al answered.

'Yes, thanks, Marj,' Wally concurred.

Marj looked at Rose in enquiry. 'No thanks. I've had enough – of food and this company.' Rose stood and left the table. Marj collected their empty plates and scurried away.

'Fancy a pint afterwards at the Dog and Duck?' Wally asked his friend.

'That would be good,' Al replied.

CHAPTER THREE

On Monday morning Esme arrived at Blue Moon to find Sonja in the office, head back in her chair with her eyes closed. Quietly, Esme tucked her handbag away in a drawer and collected the account books and pile of receipts, bills and invoices. As she sat down she noticed Sonja watching her.

'Good morning. I thought you were dozing.'

'Power napping. Not dozing.'

'Oh, of course,' Esme agreed sagely. 'You know the usual time for power napping is early afternoon, not…' she glanced at her watch, 'not ten past nine in the morning.'

'You haven't been here this weekend. If you had, you would understand.'

'Busy time?'

'The new guest arrived on Friday afternoon.'

'Oh yes. What's she like?'

Sonja shuddered. 'Your worst nightmare.'

'Surely she can't be that bad. She's only been here five minutes!'

Sonja closed her eyes again. 'You'll see, I'm sure. I've

already had her in here this morning complaining about breakfast – again. In fact, you must have just missed her.'

As Esme laid her work out and began to sort the papers Paula entered the office, carefully closing the door behind her.

'Good, you're here, Esme,' she said.

'Hello, Paula. I understand there's some trouble with the new guest?'

'Some trouble? An understatement of some magnitude. The woman is a… I can't find the right words. At least none that are suitable for polite company anyway.' She glanced over at Sonja, who still rested with closed eyes. 'I can't help here today. I promised Maria,' referring to their much-valued cook, 'I'd bake some puddings for today's lunch and cakes for tea. Then I've got a long-standing engagement to play cards this afternoon.' She looked apologetically at Sonja. 'I suppose I could cancel, but it's a bit late for the others to find a fourth.'

Esme looked puzzled. 'Why are you taking on some of Maria's work? Is she ill?'

'No, but I want to keep her. Rose has asked for a special menu and Maria is not happy with the extra work. Also, unfortunately, one of the girls told her of Rose's comments about supper last night.'

Sonja moaned.

'Exactly,' Paula agreed.

Esme looked dismayed, but before she could say anything the door swung open to admit the new resident.

'Ah, Mrs Carstairs. I'm glad you're here. Someone needs to speak to the cleaner – the small dark-haired woman. I told her my room needed re-doing and she was most impertinent.'

'Impertinent?' Paula queried.

'Yes. She told me she'd finished my room and now had others to do.'

'Well, that was no doubt true.'

'It was not true. My room is not of the standard of cleanliness I'd expect. Especially considering the rates you charge.'

Paula turned to Sonja. 'As I was telling you, I have urgent matters to attend to. Please would you go with Mrs Johns to sort this out?'

Sonja gave Paula a fulminating look before rising and following Rose out.

Paula sighed. 'I don't know what we're going to do. In just a couple of days she seems to have upset practically everyone here in one way or another.' She looked unhappily at Esme. 'It's Neil I'm most concerned about. He really shouldn't have to deal with this. I just hope his stress levels don't bring on another attack.'

Esme rose to comfort the anxious woman. 'We'll all pitch in to help. Maybe once she's settled in properly, she'll be more relaxed.'

Paula patted her hand. 'We can always hope, even if I'm pretty certain she's unlikely to change!' She stood up. 'Well, I must get to work in my kitchen.' With a small smile she sallied away.

Shortly afterwards Sonja reappeared and threw herself into her chair. 'I could kill her.'

'What was the problem?'

'A small cobweb behind the pelmet. That's all, but she wanted the whole room redone!'

'I take it you smoothed out the matter?'

'I removed the web myself and just left the room.'

'She does seem quite forceful.'

'One way of putting it!'

That evening, Esme regaled Matt with the news of the advent of Rose Johns. 'Honestly, at first I thought Sonja was exaggerating. Then she came into the office without so much as a perfunctory knock and just laid in about Jan's cleaning of her room.'

'Well, I suppose she is entitled to have a clean room.'

'It was clean! Just a teeny cobweb behind the curtain pelmet. I mean, how did she even find it? She must have climbed onto a chair to see it. Pity she didn't fall and break her neck.'

'Bit bloodthirsty, Esme!'

'Well, you should see what she's done. At breakfast and lunch the residents were huddled in their little groups. There was no chatter and laughter like there was usually.'

'Who did this Rose sit with?' Matt asked curiously.

'No one. As I said, the rest all hunkered down together. Rose sat at a table on her own. Sad, really, but understandable in a way – she's demanded her own choice of meals. She doesn't like any of the options on the general menu.'

'If she's as bad as you say, you'd be wise to keep your distance,' Matt counselled. 'These situations have a habit of suddenly boiling over and you don't want to be in the wrong place at the wrong time.'

'I know, and I'll try. But I must help the others.'

He shook his head ruefully. Always ready to help people, whether wise or not. Still, that was his Esme and, truthfully, he would not have her any other way.

❧

Meanwhile, at the Carstairs' supper table, Paula brooded. Neil was silent but clearly tense. A tension brought on by that Rose woman. Something would have to be done about her.

At intervals Selina eyed her parents. The atmosphere was terribly thick and no one was talking. She had hoped to slip in her bit of news among the general conversation – preferably just before she left the house for the rest of the evening. But clearly this was not to be. She laid down her knife and fork.

'You know the music festival planned on the beach?'

Paula looked up. 'Yes, I've read about it. There's quite a protest about it as the beach will be off-limits to the locals and the tourists unless they buy a ticket.'

'Oh really, Mum. It's not as if they're taking over the entire coast. Just a small section and it's only for three days.'

Neil roused himself. 'What about this festival?'

'Zoggo and his band are going, and I'm going with them.'

'What about your job at the coffee shop?'

'They don't mind. I've already told them.'

'I don't think it's a good idea,' Neil said.

'I didn't think you would,' Selina muttered.

'You won't be too late coming in at night, will you?' Paula hastily intervened.

'Obviously I won't be coming home each night. I'll stay there with Zoggo.'

'Don't be ridiculous,' her father expostulated. 'It's only a few miles away. Why can't you come back each night? Your mother and I will worry about you.'

'You do hear of dreadful things happening at these events. Drugs, intoxication, physical attacks. Even people dying.'

Selina frowned at her mother. 'Look on the bright side, do!'

'You do read about such things,' Paula justified herself.

'Mum, hundreds, thousands of people go to these festivals and only a very few have trouble. Of course, they're written about in the press, but no one mentions the thousands who come to no harm and just enjoy themselves and the music.'

'Think of your mother. You'd be better off earning more money ready for university.'

Selina stood so abruptly her chair fell backwards with a clatter. 'You're impossible. You never want me to have any fun.' She left the room, slamming the door behind her. Paula flinched a second time as the front door was banged closed a few moments later.

CHAPTER FOUR

How Rose found out about Larry's special arrangement with Neil was a mystery. Only three people knew of it – Larry, Neil and Esme, as she kept the accounts.

The situation was that Penny Child's stay in Blue Moon was financed by the local authority, but this covered only the bare essentials. Larry had been drawn to Penny virtually from her arrival and, once he guessed her situation, had made arrangements with Neil that the cost of any extra luxuries would be covered by him. Penny was not to know about it. Larry correctly assumed that if she had any idea about it, her embarrassment would cause her to move away. For the last year or so he had been gently courting Penny and hoped to persuade her soon to marry him. Apart from his personal feelings, it would have the added benefit that, if anything were to happen to him, her continued comfort would be assured. As his widow she would naturally inherit his money, especially as he had no close family.

Jane, Penny, Larry and Bob would often, when the weather was agreeable, take leisurely walks through the woods. On this particular occasion Rose joined them – as none of them were capable of being rude enough to deny her. At some point she attached herself to Penny and the two fell a little behind.

'So,' Rose asked archly, 'what's the position between you and Larry?'

'We're friends.'

'Really? I'd have thought you were more than that.'

Penny's cheeks turned a little pink. 'We really are just friends.'

'Mmm. I think it's more than that.'

'Well, maybe, I don't know.' She was becoming slightly flustered.

Larry glanced back and quickly discerned her discomfort. He dropped back to join them. 'Everything all right here?' He asked them both but was looking at Penny.

'Yes, of course.' But Penny's relief at his presence was palpable.

Rose concurred. 'Oh yes, everything's fine. We were just discussing your friendship. How deep it is.'

'I'm very fond of Penny.'

Rose inclined her head. 'That's obvious given how you look after her.'

'I don't mean to be rude,' Larry said, not really caring if he was, 'but is it actually any business of yours?'

'I suppose not, but it is kind of you to be so generous to Penny.'

Penny looked puzzled. 'What are you talking about?'

Larry realised Rose knew of the arrangement. 'I've no idea.' He grasped Penny's arm lightly as he turned to address the meddlesome woman. 'If you'll excuse us, Rose, I know Jane wanted to have a word with Penny.'

Rose raised her hand and let it drop. 'Off you go, then. Penny, we can finish our conversation another day.'

Not if I can prevent it, Larry thought as he and Penny hurried to catch up with the other two ahead. For the rest of the afternoon he ensured Penny and Rose were not left alone together.

When they arrived back at Blue Moon, Penny said she was tired and intended to take a nap before tea. Once he was assured she was out of Rose's reach, at least for the time being, Larry made a beeline for the office. Neil and Esme were both there and looked up at his sudden entrance.

'I thought I made it clear my arrangements concerning Penny were to be kept absolutely confidential.'

Neil got to his feet in response to the other man's barely contained fury. 'It is. Only the three of us know.'

'That's where you're wrong. Rose Johns knows.'

Neil was shocked. 'I certainly didn't tell her, or anyone else for that matter – including my wife. And I know I can vouch for Esme.'

Esme nodded.

'Well, how did she find out?'

Neil shook his head, perplexed. 'I can't understand it. Do you want me to speak to Rose?'

'No.' Larry was calming down. 'It would probably just make matters worse. I'll speak to her.'

No one knew exactly what transpired between Larry and Rose, but it appeared to quash her intention to tell Penny, at least for the time being. However, Larry was no fool and made it his business the two women were kept as far apart as possible.

Having been apparently thwarted on one front, Rose turned her attention in another direction. Celia Foster and Lucy Strong had met at secretarial college in their teens and been best friends since then. Rose spied them in a tea shop in the village a few days later and went in.

'Fancy seeing you two here. Mind if I join you?' Without waiting for a reply she drew out a chair and sat down, ostensibly not noticing their lack of welcome.

To start with the conversation was innocuous, even banal. Then Rose asked, 'So you two have been friends all your lives?'

'Since we were seventeen, yes,' Celia confirmed.

'You seem to do everything together.'

'We enjoy each other's company, if that's what you mean.' Celia's tone was frosty.

Lucy piped in, 'There's nothing wrong with that.'

Rose waited for her tea to be placed in front of her, then poured herself a cup of the Earl Grey. 'Nothing at all. It must be nice for you both to be so close.'

Neither woman answered her. After taking a bite of her slice of Battenburg and eating it, Rose raised her napkin to dab her lips free from any stray crumb. 'Almost like a married couple.'

'There's nothing wrong with our friendship.' Lucy sounded agitated.

'You're right,' Rose agreed. 'You are both lucky to have such a close bond.'

Lucy's face was suffused with red. 'We're not lesbians.' Her raised voice attracted attention from nearby tables and she slumped back, looking miserable.

Softly, Rose said, 'I didn't say you were. But now that you mention it…'

Lucy looked at her friend. Despite her name, she was the more sensitive of the two. Celia was the more pragmatic, but she was fiercely protective of her friend. She addressed Rose, 'You're not the first to infer that, but you're wrong.'

Rose was looking at Lucy's visible distress. 'Am I?'

Celia's tone was firm. 'Yes. I know there's no stigma

attached to being gay, as it's termed nowadays, even if we were. But in the past there have been such allusions made when it was generally thought to be freakish. Lucy had a bad experience when a rumour started about us at her work. That's why she gets so upset about it.' She stood up. 'Come on, Lucy, it's time for us to leave.'

Rose smiled maliciously as she watched the two friends pay for their unfinished tea and leave the shop.

So harmony was just a distant memory at Blue Moon by the time the next meeting of the Residents' Association arrived. Everyone was entitled, indeed encouraged, to attend, and most did. Wally and Al skipped a few, while Charles rarely put in an appearance. On this occasion, however, it was a full house.

Alice, as chair, opened the proceedings by welcoming Rose to her first meeting. There were a few general murmurs but before Alice could continue Rose spoke up. 'Who is taking the minutes?'

No one immediately answered, then Alice ventured, 'We don't have minutes – most of us attend regularly and it's easy to tell anyone who does miss a meeting anything they should know.'

'So there's no record kept?'

Peter intervened. 'Not a formal one, no.'

Rose tried another angle. 'What is in the Association's constitution?'

'I don't think…' Alice faltered.

This time it was Wally who spoke up. 'There is no constitution. There's no need. This is an informal forum.'

Rose looked amazed. 'What exactly is its remit then?'

Wally again answered, 'It's a chance to sort out any small problems that could affect some or all of us. Also, trips and entertainments are planned.'

Rose peered across at him. 'This is the most ridiculous group I've ever encountered.'

After a small silence, Al reminded her, 'You don't have to attend, if you don't want to.'

Rose sniffed and turned back to Alice. 'When were you elected as chair?'

'I wasn't. Not really.'

Peter added, 'Alice kindly volunteered.'

'And she's done a good job.' Wally smiled at Alice.

'I give up,' Rose declared. 'I've never come across such a set-up before. No proper organisation, no proper election of officers, so patently undemocratic. I don't see its value.'

Alice looked close to tears. Some of the residents were talking sotto voce to their neighbour. Peter faced down Rose. 'You know its value, Wally explained it to you. If it doesn't meet your requirements, I suggest you leave.'

Rose stared back at him. After a few moments, she turned to Alice. 'Complaints. I have several I'd like you to formally take to Neil. I've already spoken to him but nothing has improved.'

Alice picked up her pen. 'What is your complaint?'

'Complaints. As I said, I have a number of them.' She then proceeded to list her dissatisfaction with the menus, waitress service, Sonja's attitude, the standard of cleaning – the list seemed to go on and on while Alice dutifully took notes.

Once she finished, no one appeared to have any appetite to extend the meeting, which accordingly broke up. Rose was the first to sweep out of the room, with the others soon following. Alice and Peter were the only two left.

'I suppose she's right, in a way,' Alice conceded in a small voice.

'No, she isn't. It would be ridiculous to have constitutions, mission statements and all that garbage for our little committee.'

Alice smiled at his belligerent tone. 'I know what you're saying but… I can't help feeling she did make some valid points.' She gathered up her pens and papers, looking sad again. 'I never was elected.'

'Neither was I as your deputy. And, as Wally said, it doesn't mean we don't do a good job.'

'Yes, I suppose so.' Her voice was doubtful.

'Look. Tell you what. I'll put together some notes about today's meeting. We could start keeping an informal record of what we discuss.'

'You're a good man, Peter. I don't know what I'd do without you. Well, I'd better go to the office with all these grievances.'

Alice knocked, then entered as Neil's voice answered.

'Hello, Alice.' Neil smiled. 'How did your meeting go?'

'I need to talk with you about that, but first, here is a list of complaints that Rose wanted me to give you.' She handed it over.

'Would you prefer to be in private?' Esme offered. Felicia, Neil's personal assistant, had taken some leave, so it had been just Neil and Esme in the office. 'I can go to rattle up a cup of tea or something.'

'No need for that,' Alice said. 'I just want to tell you, Neil, that I think I should step down as chair.'

Her eyes welled up; Esme quickly urged her on to a chair while Neil simply asked, 'Why?'

The floodgates opened and while not everything was intelligible, Neil and Esme were able to grasp the gist. Once Alice had calmed somewhat, Neil spoke. 'No one else agreed with her, did they?'

'No, but—'

'You do a wonderful job and I know – because the other guests have told me on various occasions.'

'But, democratically—'

'If you want to have an election, I'm sure the others will vote for you to continue.'

'I don't think I should stand.'

'Well,' Neil was bracing, 'if you don't stand, I'm not sure anyone else would – except maybe Rose herself.'

'Oh.'

'And how popular do you think that would be?'

Alice considered this. 'You really think I should carry on?'

'I do,' he replied gravely.

'Peter did say he'd write some notes on the meeting. Maybe Rose will see that as a step in the right direction.'

'That's settled, then.' Neil went back to his desk. 'And I'll deal with these complaints.'

❧

That evening Esme regaled Matt with the continuing saga of Rose at the Blue Moon. 'Maria, the cook, not to mention both Marj and Jan, are upset. Neil's really worried in case any – or, worst-case scenario, all – decide to leave. They would be difficult to replace.'

Matt chewed while he ruminated. 'Something should be done to settle things. A woman like that causes resentment. And that can ferment until Blue Moon has a catastrophe on their hands.'

'You think someone might decide to kill Rose?'

'I think you shouldn't sound so hopeful! No, I expect she'll settle down eventually and all this will blow over.'

'I hope so. And I hope it's soon for the sake of Neil's blood pressure. Paula's really worried about him.' Esme began to collect their empty plates and clear the table.

CHAPTER FIVE

The Residents' Association held another meeting the following week. It had been mooted a couple of months previously that the residents put on some sort of entertainment to celebrate the tenth anniversary of Blue Moon as a retirement home.

Alice, with a nervous glance at Rose, opened the proceedings. 'As you all know, we decided to do something to mark Blue Moon's first decade. Everyone was to try to think of ideas, so I hope you've all got suggestions.' She looked at Peter, who sat beside her, ready with a pen poised to make notes. He smiled reassurance at her. She looked round. 'Who wants to start?'

There was no immediate response, but then Jane piped up. 'We wondered about writing and performing a short play that would include some of the amusing episodes over the years.'

'Has anyone been here since its inception?' Rose queried.

'None of us,' answered Bob. 'But Sonja has and, of course, Paula. We could mine them for interesting events.'

Celia spoke up. 'Lucy wondered about a concert. You know, with turns. Singing, playing music, telling jokes – like an old-fashioned revue.'

Wally harrumphed to gain attention. 'Al and I came up with the idea of having a party. Invite friends from the village or family members if you prefer.'

There was utter silence. The concept of the two most taciturn of men suggesting a party was just too incredulous to be easily believed. Alice pulled herself together. 'Did you get all those ideas down?' she asked Peter, who nodded. 'Well, then, let's all mull them over and get back here tomorrow afternoon so we can decide which option to choose.'

Rose spoke then. 'What trite ideas – a play, a concert or a party.'

Peter answered, 'I notice you didn't put forward any ideas.'

'No, I didn't. Unlike all of you, I only heard about this at the start of this meeting. You can be sure if I'd had months to think about it, I'd have come up with some interesting suggestions.'

A few rumblings could be heard. Alice, to prevent an imminent verbal fight, quickly reiterated, 'So, we'll all meet here tomorrow. Rose, naturally if you have any proposals by then, they can be included in the discussion.'

Fracas avoided, everyone stood and filed out, all but Rose giving Alice supportive smiles. Wally, passing behind her, even laid a hand on her shoulder. 'Well done,' he said gruffly.

❧❧

As it transpired, Rose was not at the next day's meeting.

Sonja abruptly woke up. Disorientated for a few seconds, she then realised it was an alarm. Each guest had one in their room to use to call for help if they were in distress. Sonja checked the panel and groaned. It was Rose Johns. Sonja was a fully trained and experienced nurse. That was why she lived on the top floor of Blue Moon so as to be on hand for emergencies, day or night. Like now.

She got out of bed and wrapped her dressing gown round herself, tying the belt. She picked up her medical kit on the way out. Jogging down the stairs, she was soon at Rose's room. Inside it was dark and she could hear moans.

'It's me, Sonja, Rose. I'm going to put on the light in your bathroom so I can see what I'm doing.' This she did and then approached the bed. 'What is the problem, Rose?'

'I'm dying,' Rose snapped back before groaning again.

'Where's the pain?'

Rose indicated her chest. Sonja set about trying to discover the problem, which was not easy. Rose was uncooperative, as was to be expected, and full of complaints, also to be expected. Sonja made herself rise above it all as it was clear that Rose really was suffering.

Finally, she sat down, facing Rose. 'I'm not absolutely sure what the problem is, so I'm going to phone our doctor, and ask him to examine you.'

'It's obvious. I'm having a heart attack. You should be calling for an ambulance, not a local doctor.'

'One thing I'm pretty sure of is that you are not having a heart attack.'

'A lot you know,' Rose groused before hissing in a breath as the pain again surged.

When Dr Hugh Sanders arrived Sonja was waiting downstairs to let him in. 'I'm sorry to call you out so early,' she apologised. 'But difficult as Rose Johns may be, she really is in pain.'

'Don't worry.' He smiled. 'I'm grateful for any reason you ask me to come over.'

Sonja blushed and hurriedly turned to lead the way to Rose's room. She took the opportunity to describe her findings regarding Rose's problem.

They entered the room to find Rose watching for their arrival. 'About time you got here, Doctor. I need an ambulance, but this woman insists I see you first. I'll be dead before I can get any proper treatment.'

'No need to think about that.' Hugh set about his own examination after reading Sonja's notes. At least Rose was more cooperative this time.

At the end of it she eyed the doctor. 'Well? Are you sending me to hospital now?'

'No, I agree with Mrs Davies. I think your problem is wind—'

'Wind! I might have known. You medical people always stick together.'

'Mrs Johns,' Hugh intervened, 'you are definitely not having a heart attack. Wind, particularly when severe, as in your case, is extremely uncomfortable.'

'Uncomfortable? It's more than uncomfortable. It's bloody agony.'

'I'm leaving some medicine with Mrs Davies for you,' Hugh continued as if there had been no interruption. 'It's strong and fast-working. If it does not significantly relieve your pain over the next twenty-four hours, I will reassess the situation.'

'I want a second opinion – and not from a partner in your practice. I want a consultant.'

Hugh spent some time reassuring Rose, explaining

heart attack symptoms and their difference to her case. Sonja gave her a dose of the medication he had prescribed and eventually Rose calmed down, although still muttering beneath her breath as they left the room.

'You'd better keep a watchful eye on her,' Hugh warned. 'If she deteriorates or even if she makes no progress, please call me.'

'I will.' Sonja started to return to Rose, as Hugh was familiar enough with Blue Moon to find his own way out but was brought to a halt as he gently grasped her arm.

'There's an Alan Bennett play on in Brighton this week that I think you'd enjoy. Will you come with me on Friday or Saturday evening?'

She smiled. 'Hugh, we've been over this so many times. It just wouldn't work.'

'I disagree. Oh, I know we're colleagues here. But I'm asking you to get away from here and come with me to the theatre for one evening. There's really no valid reason we shouldn't see each other in our spare time.'

'Hugh,' she looked down at his hand still lightly holding her arm, 'it's not just the "colleagues" thing, as you know. I'm several years older than you.'

He released her arm. 'Not the age difference thing again. It's only a few years.'

'But—'

'And, I'd like to point out, both your children have given their blessing.'

'Blessing! They practically nag me!'

'Well then?'

'I'm sorry. It just doesn't feel right to me.'

Resigned, he accepted her decision but warned, 'Don't think I won't wear you down eventually! I'm nothing if not persistent.'

'Ain't that the truth.' She laughed, relieved their friendship still appeared to be intact. She returned to Rose's room to be brought straight back to earth.

'What were you and the doc talking about? Getting your stories to match?'

Sonja sighed as she set about trying to make her irascible patient more comfortable.

During the next couple of days Blue Moon regained some of its pre-Rose harmony – at least as far as the residents were concerned. It was not so harmonious for Sonja nursing Rose in her bedroom, although she did have periods of respite when either Paula or Esme stood in for her. However, the time came when she was fully recovered and ready to rejoin everyone else downstairs.

On her entry into the lounge there was not much welcome. Only Alice stood and approached her. 'How are you feeling?'

Rose swept a derisive look in her direction. 'Obviously better or I wouldn't be here.'

Flushed with embarrassment, Alice returned to her chair, where Peter saw her settled after sending a fulminating glare at the other woman.

Undeterred, Rose crossed to where a small group were listening to the news on the radio. She sat next to Bob Pargeter. 'Really, that Alice. Queen of Banality or,' her voice took on a considering tone, 'Queen of Stupidity maybe.'

No one responded, apparently engrossed in the report of a contentious debate in Parliament.

Shortly afterwards, Lucy and Celia came into the lounge and passed nearby the radio group on their way to a bay window seat. Rose pursed her lips as they passed. 'I'm sure they do share an unnatural relationship,' she observed to no one in particular. She smiled when Lucy coloured. Celia turned, obviously intent on taking issue, but her friend grabbed her hand and hurried across to the window.

Penny leant forward to address Rose. 'Do you mind? We're trying to listen to this report.'

Rose fixed a gimlet stare at her. 'Well, you're pretty lucky to be here.'

'What does that mean?'

'Why, only that Larry here is a good friend to you.'

'Yes, he is.' Penny was clearly confused.

'A very good, generous friend to you.' Rose's tone was rife with meaning.

Penny looked from Rose to Larry. She was aware there was a subtext but could not fathom it.

Abruptly Larry stood and switched off the radio. As the others stared at him, he said, 'Can't concentrate on it, anyway.' He turned to Penny. 'Come on, Pen, we'll have a stroll before supper.'

Rose laughed.

'Witch,' Larry muttered as he hauled a bewildered Penny towards the door.

Once they had disappeared, Rose turned to Bob. 'Everyone here seems to pair off. What do you think of the relationship between that Alice woman and Peter?'

'I think it's none of my business, nor of yours either.' He got up and left. After a moment or two of hesitation, Jane followed him out.

Undeterred at being left alone, Rose moved across to where Alice and Peter were sitting. Alice eyed her nervously, but before she could speak Rose said, 'Have you passed on my comments to management on the need for better cleaning?'

Alice nodded. 'Yes. That same day, in fact.'

'Well, no action seems to have been taken that I can see.'

Alice, uncharacteristically brave, responded, 'No one else has complained. They all seem to be satisfied with the conditions here.'

Rose gave a meaningful look in Peter's direction, then turned back to Alice. 'A lot of them have transparently low standards, while some seem to be pretty gutless.'

'What do you mean?'

'Yes,' Peter's voice was hard, 'what do you mean?'

Rose shrugged. 'It's quite clear to me there are a couple of men here too chicken to speak out. For instance, some people not only lack money but also a backbone.' She looked hard and steady into Peter's eyes for a few moments. Then she turned back to Alice. 'As I say, some people here have pretty low standards. However, I do not. The cleaning is slapdash. The staff should be reprimanded and told to do better if they don't want to lose their jobs.' Oblivious, or apparently oblivious, she walked towards the window, chose an armchair near to Charles, extracted a book from her bag and began to read.

Meanwhile, in the annex Neil and Selina were in the midst of another argument on the same old themes.

Paula, returning from playing bridge, hurried inside. 'For goodness' sake, I could hear you two from the car park.'

'Dad started going on about Zoggo again.'

'All I said, and I'll repeat it, is that Zoggo is at the root of her wanting to throw her life away.'

'I'm not throwing it away. I'm going to university next year, aren't I?'

'To study music. With your brains, you should be taking a degree in something that will form a sturdy base for a successful career.'

'Oh, my, God.' Selina threw her hands up in frustration.

Her father continued, 'Zoggo dropped out of university, abandoned an economics degree and now mooches off other people while he makes a din he calls music. And you admire him! No wonder I worry about his influence over you!'

'I give up. You just don't understand.'

Neil abruptly stood and left the room, muttering very audibly, 'I understand, all right.'

Paula looked at her daughter. 'You should remember your dad's state of health. It's not good for him to be upset like this.'

'You're always on his side!' Selina stormed out of the house.

❦

That evening over supper, Esme regaled Matt about the toxic atmosphere at Blue Moon. 'Perhaps because I'm not there every day, it's very noticeable. Also, while Rose Johns was safely tucked away with her wind, the whole place relaxed and it was almost like old times.'

'I thought you hated your spells with Rose, when you relieved Sonja?'

'Yes, I did. But I knew it was just for a set period of time. I'm talking about the other guests. They've been so tense, but with Rose out of the picture things were getting back to normal. Then she came downstairs today and the atmosphere immediately changed. She managed to upset several of the guests within about half an hour!'

'You saw this?' Matt was sceptical.

'Not directly, no. But I saw Charles when I was leaving. He told me. Funny, really,' her tone became pensive, 'he's one to keep to himself usually. Spends a lot of time watching the others and analysing their behaviour. Just the fact that he talked to me shows how disturbed he is by her.'

'I don't know. Seems to me a lot of people confide in you.'

Esme finished her last mouthful. 'I think it's affecting Neil too. He and his daughter had a humdinger of an argument this afternoon. Everyone could hear them shouting at each other.'

'Everyone?' Matt murmured.

'Well, we had the window open in the office and we could hear them quite clearly. I'm just glad I'm not there full-time – day and night!'

'Believe me, so am I.'

CHAPTER SIX

Late on Wednesday night, Celia and Lucy returned to Blue Moon after spending the evening at a concert followed by a scrumptious meal at the Red Lion. Both had enjoyed the evening enormously but by the time the taxi deposited them at the front door, their excitement had morphed into a pleasant weariness. Celia unlocked the door, stepped inside, switched on the light then turned, ready to close and lock the door once Lucy had followed her in.

A sharp indrawn breath made Celia glance at her friend. Seeing her horrified expression and fixed stare towards the stairs, she swung round to see what had caught her attention.

'Oh my God.' She hurried over.

'Is she dead?' Lucy, who had not moved from just inside the door, quavered.

'I'm not sure. Unconscious certainly.' She saw Lucy was starting to break down and put some command in her voice as she continued, 'I'll stay here. You go and rattle up Sonja.'

'Oh dear.' Lucy scuttled passed with her face averted and hurried up the stairs.

As she disappeared, Celia looked down at the sprawled figure at the foot of the stairs. 'Did you manage to upset someone so much you pushed them over the edge, Rose? Or did you fall accidentally?'

Receiving no reply, she sat in one of the hall's Jacobean-style carver chairs while waiting for Sonja. Very shortly she arrived and immediately knelt by Rose. After a brief examination she breathed a sigh of relief and stood up, collected an afghan from the back of the sofa and laid it over the prone Rose.

'She's still alive, thank goodness. Although not in the best condition. Can you remain with her while I call for the doctor?'

'Of course.'

'Good, I won't be long.' Sonja hurried to the office.

Celia heard voices and looked up to see Lucy and Peter coming down the stairs. Lucy remained on the bottom step, gripping the banister, while Peter, after a long look at Rose, moved over to where Celia was sitting, frowning at Lucy.

'Don't blame her,' he said. 'I woke up to hear running footsteps, then a few minutes later more footsteps going in the opposite direction. So I got up to see what was going on.'

Celia nodded. 'And when you opened your door, Lucy was passing,' she said in a resigned tone.

'You've got it. Lucy said Rose was dead?'

'Sonja says not. She's in the office now calling for the doctor.'

Lucy nearly stepped forward only to freeze where she was as she recollected Rose's straggled body. 'Not dead?'

Celia went over to her. 'No, just unconscious. The doctor will be coming and everything is going to take some time. Why don't you go on up to your room?'

'I couldn't possibly go to sleep!'

'No, probably not. But you could try to relax. Play some of your favourite music.'

'But—'

'Really, Lucy. You can't help here.'

'Well—'

Peter intervened, 'Why don't you accompany her upstairs? I'll stay here until you return.'

Celia hesitated momentarily, her eyes going to the closed office door before taking Lucy's arm to turn her round and encourage her to leave the hall. 'Thanks. I'll be back as quickly as possible.' She was as good as her word and only a few minutes passed before she was back.

Sonja emerged from the office. 'Dr Saunders is on his way. Peter, what are you doing here?'

He explained again of hearing disturbances and coming to investigate. 'I'll be off back to bed,' he finished.

Sonja sighed as he disappeared and she glanced down at her dressing gown. 'It's an imposition, I know, but can I ask you to stay on here while I just run up to put on some more suitable clothes? If Dr Saunders decides to send Rose to hospital, I'll need to go with her. Also, I should let Neil know what's happened.'

'No problem.' Celia returned to her carver and reseated herself.

When Hugh Saunders arrived there was just Sonja waiting with Rose. He knelt to examine the stricken woman but rose shortly. He looked at Sonja soberly. 'She's dead.'

'What? But there was definitely a pulse when I looked at her.'

'I don't doubt it,' he soothed.

'If there hadn't been I'd have called for an ambulance straight away… and the police.'

He encouraged her to sit down. 'Calm yourself. She

hasn't been dead long, I would estimate she died between our two examinations.'

'Yes.' She worked to get a grip on herself.

'I'll ring the police and for an ambulance.' Hugh tactfully left her alone as he withdrew into the office.

❧

Later that morning in the police station, Frank Shute called Matt and his partner, Rick, into his office.

'Sudden death late last night or early this morning. Police Constable Travers attended, you can get the details from him. Looks like an accident. Old lady fell down some stairs. Travers was thorough, talked to the doctor on scene, as well as the paramedics. And there was also some sort of residential nurse.'

Matt felt a sinking feeling develop. 'Where was this, sir?'

Shute glanced down at his notes. 'Blue Moon old people's home, on the outskirts of town.'

'A select home for those in their twilight years,' Matt muttered.

'What's that?'

'Oh, sorry, sir. Esme does some bookkeeping there and that's how she describes it.'

'That's as may be. You'll need to go out there and talk to those involved in finding the body.'

'Travers didn't get their statements?'

'Apparently the two guests who found the body had gone to bed. And the resident nurse flatly refused to disturb them. I gather one of them is rather sensitive and had been greatly upset.' Shute sounded slightly aggrieved.

Matt smiled. 'Right, we'll get on to it, sir.'

'Don't forget to talk with Travers first. Naturally, he had his lapel camera running while he was there, so his report is detailed. However, as an accident, it should be pretty much an open and closed case.'

'What was the name of the deceased?' Matt asked.

Checking the notes in front of him, Shute replied, 'Rose Johns.'

'Should have guessed,' Matt said to his partner as they went in search of the police constable who had attended the scene.

'Guessed?'

'Yeah. From Esme. This Rose Johns has only recently started living there but apparently has managed to upset practically everyone in the place – whether fellow resident or staff.'

'Oh. So it may not have been an accident?'

Matt shrugged. 'We'll have to see, but what are the odds that a person universally disliked dies by accident?'

'Not great, I suppose.'

After seeing Travers the two men made their way to the morgue. They could have phoned, but John Meadows, although an excellent medical examiner, could be a tad taciturn, not to mention irritable, when asked about one of his cases before he had finished his post-mortem and written up his findings. In these circumstances, face-to-face encounters were more likely to produce results. They found him in his cubicle which masqueraded as an office. He was immaculately turned out as always, even when he was called out in the middle of the night. Matt privately hypothesised that the man never slept, just waited fully dressed for a call-out.

John looked up and frowned as they entered. 'What are you doing here?'

'Morning, John,' Matt said affably as he sat in the only remaining chair, leaving Rick to prop himself against the wall.

'Morning. What are you doing here?'

'We wanted anything you've got on Rose Johns – fell downstairs last night at Blue Moon Residential Home.'

'You're too early. I haven't started on her yet.'

'I'm here for your impressions after your preliminary examination in situ last night.'

'Last night? Early hours this morning, you mean.'

'Yes.'

Realising he was not going to be left alone to get on with his work until he gave them what he had so far, Meadows put down his pen with care and clasped his hands.

'She fell down the stairs, broke several bones. Apparently she was still alive, although unconscious, between eleven-fifteen and eleven-thirty when she was first found. However, by the time the doctor arrived at approximately midnight, she had died.'

After a pause, Matt realised the medical examiner had finished. 'Any idea of when she fell?'

'I'm not a miracle worker nor a seer. Look you've got a pretty accurate time of her actual death. Before a post-mortem I can only surmise she fell by accident and that the fall caused her death. I'm not committing any further until I have all the information her body will yield.'

'Okay, thanks, John.' Matt stood up. 'Can you tell me when you'll be doing the PM?'

'She's not the only one I have waiting, you know.'

'Yeah. It's just that if you can confirm conclusively it was an accident, we can close the case quickly.'

John looked at Matt with shrewd eyes. 'You have any reason not to think it accidental?'

'Not exactly. More a feeling.'

'I see.' He stared at the ceiling while he thought. 'All right. I have a few doubts myself. I'll bump her up the list a bit.'

'Thanks.'

'Don't bother me again until my report is finished.'

Matt nodded and he left with Rick as John picked up his pen and resumed his work.

When the detectives arrived at Blue Moon they were met by Neil, who ushered them into the office.

'I understand you wish to speak with the two residents who found Rose. I've warned them and asked them to make themselves available.'

'Thank you, Mr Carstairs. We also would like to talk with Sonja Davies.'

'She's around somewhere. I can find her for you, but the policeman here last night did question her. I'm not sure she'll have anything further to add.'

'Yes, we've seen his report but would just like to clarify a couple of matters.'

'Of course.' Neil glanced round the office. 'Would you like to see them in here?'

'That would be convenient, thank you.'

Neil moved nearer to the door, where he paused. 'I would be grateful if you didn't upset any of them.'

'We'll do our best not to,' Matt replied gravely.

'It's just that Lucy Strong, one of the residents who first found Rose, has a particularly sensitive nature. Last night took quite a toll on her.'

'I'll bear that in mind. Perhaps, in that case, we should talk with her first. Less time for her to worry about it.'

Neil smiled in gratitude and left to fetch Lucy.

Rick snorted. 'I felt like saying what a shame we left

our waterboarding equipment and finger-breaking pliers behind!'

Matt smiled in appreciation but pointed out, 'He's only trying to protect his charges.' He clicked on his lapel recorder as Rick did the same. All interviews outside the police station were recorded in this way. However, Matt still liked Rick to take full notes, while he himself usually jotted down key points that struck him. Although not strictly necessary, Matt liked a back-up in case of technology failure – which had been known to happen. Also, interviewees were usually more relaxed with overt notetaking rather than dwelling on the fact that every word said was being recorded.

At a timid knock, Rick opened the door to admit a slim figure with very short silver hair shaped close to the contours of her head.

'Please come in and sit down,' Matt invited.

This she did, but on the edge of the chair with a tense ramrod-straight back. 'Dreadful business,' she murmured as Rick seated himself ready to take notes.

'Indeed. I wonder if you could tell me exactly what happened last night?'

She hesitated. 'Where should I start?'

'I understand you had been out for the evening?'

'Oh, yes.' There was a small but visible relaxation. 'We – that is, Celia and I – went to a concert in town. It was very good. Of course, the orchestra is well established, but the conductor, Max Bloch – I think he's Austrian, or is it German?' She paused to ponder.

Matt cleared his throat.

'Oh, yes, I suppose that doesn't matter. Anyway, he's not so well known yet. But I'm sure he will be.'

'After the concert?' Matt prompted.

'Oh, afterwards we treated ourselves to dinner at the

Red Lion. It was really very good and we had some wine as well.' She had a moment of pleasant recollection, then her smile slipped as she continued, 'We got a taxi back here. It was late but Celia had taken a key to the front door and she let us in. As soon as she turned on the light, I saw her – Rose, I mean – on the floor.' She pulled her cardigan tight around herself. 'Awful.'

'Yes, I can understand,' Matt sympathised gently. 'Did you or your friend move or touch her in any way?'

'No.' Revulsion clear in her voice.

'All right. That's good. What happened then?'

'Celia told me to fetch Sonja. She's a nurse, you know.'

Matt nodded.

'So I went up to call her and she came down here. Then on my way back I met Peter and we came down together.'

'Peter?'

'Yes. Peter Francis. He came out of his room as I was passing. We came down together. I don't think Celia was particularly pleased to see him. But what could I do?'

'Then?'

'Then? Oh, yes, Celia said Rose wasn't dead, just unconscious – such a relief I felt, I remember – and Sonja was calling Dr Saunders.' She paused, thinking. 'After that Celia took me to my room. She didn't want me to stay downstairs.' There was a hint of resentment in her voice.

'And that was that? You didn't come downstairs again?'

'No. I got ready for bed and put some music on and sat in my armchair. I must have drifted off and I didn't wake until it was nearly time to get up. Then, at breakfast, we were all told Rose had died!'

'Must have been a shock.' Matt paused for a brief moment. 'Thank you, Miss Strong, for such a clear account of events.'

Glowing from his praise Lucy floated out while Rick sought out Celia Foster. As she appeared, Matt was struck by the dissimilarity between the two friends. Celia had a sturdy physique with long brown hair, harshly streaked with grey and severely pulled back into a French twist.

She breezed in, sat down and eyed Matt appraisingly. 'Are you Esme's Matt?'

Caught off-guard, he stiffened before nodding. 'Yes.' He chose not to notice Rick's grin.

'I wondered. Esme's told us about you.'

Slightly unnerved, Matt decided to get this interview back on track. 'Right. About last night, will you tell me what happened? You and Miss Strong were out?'

'Yes, we went to a concert. The orchestra was led by an up-and-coming conductor, Max Bloch. Very good. Then we had a meal at the Red Lion and afterwards got a taxi back. It was late so everything was locked up, but Neil had given me a key. When we got in, there was Rose at the foot of the stairs. Lucy was getting upset so I sent her to fetch Sonja, who came really quite quickly. She checked Rose and said she wasn't dead so she would call the doctor.'

'Anything else?'

'No, I don't think so.'

'Did Miss Strong return to the hall?'

'Oh, yes... and with Peter Francis. He can be a bit of a busybody. Anyway, I took Lucy up to her room and returned to the hall as Sonja had asked me to keep an eye on Rose. In case she regained consciousness, I suppose. Then,' she squinted in thought, 'Peter went back upstairs. Sonja went to put on some clothes in case she needed to accompany Rose to the hospital and I think she popped over to the annexe to inform Neil of the accident. When she got back I left her to wait for the doctor.'

'Thank you, Miss Foster. You've been most helpful and succinct.' As the door closed behind her, Matt said to his partner, 'At least their stories tally.'

There was a short knock before Neil poked his head in. 'I know you wanted to see Mrs Sonja Davies, but apparently she's gone to bed. I'm loath to wake her as she was up for hours last night – or, technically, I suppose, this morning – and was completely exhausted.'

The two detectives exchanged glances. 'No, that's all right, but we will have to see her. I know she gave a statement earlier, but there are a couple of things we'd like to confirm.'

'Yes, I see. Well, thank you. When she gets up, I'll ask her to contact you.'

'Good.' Matt handed over his card with contact details. 'In the meantime, perhaps we could hear your version of events?'

'Of course.' He sat down. 'Sonja – Mrs Davies – came to the annexe, where I live with my family, to wake and tell me of the accident. I put on some clothes and came over. Dr Saunders was here, in the office, calling for an ambulance and the police. Sonja was very upset. I gather from her initial examination, Rose was alive with a reasonably steady pulse, albeit unconscious and with obvious broken bones. That was why she didn't move her. But when the doctor came, he declared Rose dead. I assume her heart gave out with the shock.'

'We'll know the actual cause of death from the post-mortem.'

'Of course. Of course. Anyhow, Sonja was pretty upset. Then, well, then the ambulance arrived and your man.'

After thanking him for his cooperation and use of the office, Matt asked, 'Is Peter Francis about?' However, after a search, Neil surmised he had accompanied some of the others on an expedition to the village.

'Not to worry,' Matt assured him. 'We'll come back tomorrow. Perhaps both he and Mrs Davies will be available then?'

'Certainly Sonja Davies and I'll do my best regarding Peter Francis.'

❧

That evening, for once it was Matt with news of Blue Moon. 'Esme, guess where I was today?'

She looked puzzled. 'Today?'

'Yes. I was at Blue Moon.'

'Whatever for? What happened? Matt, don't keep me in suspense!'

He relented. 'One of the residents had an accident – unfortunately a fatal one. So, naturally, we had to be called in.'

'Fatal? Oh God, who was it?'

Matt drew out the suspense by taking a couple of swallows of his beer. 'Rose Johns.'

'Oh.'

'That's it? Oh?'

'Well, I shouldn't speak ill of the dead…'

'But you're going to anyway!'

'It's just if it had to happen to any of them, she would be my choice. What happened?'

'It looks as if she fell down the main stairs.'

'Not a nice way to go.'

'No. Although I understand she was unconscious and so at least not in pain.'

'It would happen on a day I don't go there.'

'Esme, I'm not at all sure that is a correct sentiment.'

'Phooey. I'd only say it to you.'

'And that makes it all right?'

'Yes!' She smiled beguilingly at him.

He laughed.

CHAPTER SEVEN

Everything changed the next morning when Matt received a phone call at the station. It was John Meadows.

'I thought I should let you know as soon as possible. Although I haven't yet done a full post-mortem on your Rose Johns, I took note of your "feeling" yesterday along with my own niggles.'

'Yes?'

'Your instinct was right. According to my preliminary findings, she did not die accidentally. She may, or may not, have fallen by accident – I'll be able to tell you more after a full examination. However, the actual cause of death was asphyxiation. Her lips, ears and fingernails showed a faint bluish tinge. Additionally, she had petechiae in the eyes.'

'Petech…?'

'Burst blood capillaries to the layman.'

'Wouldn't there have been marks on her neck and facial signs?'

'Yes, but she wasn't strangled, she was smothered.'

'Smothered?'

'Yes, most likely with a pillow or cushion.' Meadows

sounded testy at the interruption. 'Anyway, I thought you needed to know she was murdered for your investigation. My full report will follow after I've done a complete post-mortem.'

'Thank you,' Matt said, although Meadows had rung off so abruptly it was unlikely he had heard. He looked at his partner. 'We're now investigating a murder, not an accident.' He got up and headed for the SIO's office.

Frank Shute heard him out. 'Well, you'd better take SOCO with you. They can extend their investigation, for what it's worth now that umpteen people have no doubt wandered all over the scene and contaminated it. But at least they may be able to find the actual murder weapon.'

'Sir.' Matt returned to his desk.

'Before we go back to Blue Moon,' he said to Rick, 'I want to start up our incident board. Put everything on it we have from Travers and the interviews yesterday.'

They mostly worked in silence until Rick said, 'I suppose this makes the similarity of the events as described by Celia Foster and Lucy Strong a bit suspect rather than convenient, as we thought yesterday.'

Matt shrugged. 'Yes, it could do. Although Miss Strong's statement was a bit scattered and not as a rehearsed account would sound.'

'Not to mention if she would be capable of keeping to a set script!'

Matt grinned. 'There is that.'

The two detectives arrived at Blue Moon over the lunch period. This was a deliberate ploy based on the premise that, according to Esme, most of the residents ate in for the main meal of the day. So they would be available for questioning.

On their way towards the office they passed Lucy

Strong. They nodded a greeting and would have continued except she reached out to touch Matt's arm. 'If I'd known you were Esme's Matt, I wouldn't have been a bit worried about talking to you. She's told us so much about you.'

'I see.' Matt was nonplussed. 'Well, that's very kind of you to say so.'

She smiled and continued on to the dining room while Matt, hearing Rick's snort of laughter, warned, 'Not a word – neither now nor at any time in the future.'

He knocked on the office door and on receiving a reply walked in followed by his smirking partner.

Neil welcomed them and bade them sit down before saying somewhat reproachfully, 'I've had Peter Francis on stand-by for you all morning.'

'Thank you, Mr Carstairs. However, circumstances have changed. Rose Johns, we now know, did not die as a result of an accident. She was deliberately killed, presumably by someone living here.'

'Killed! Deliberately. I can't believe it. Who by?'

'Well, that is the question we will be working towards finding the answer to.' Matt smiled genially. 'Of course we do still want to speak with Mr Francis and, as he's been waiting all morning, we can start with him. But we will need to interview everybody now. Everyone who is connected to this place.'

'I see.' Neil collapsed against the back of his chair. 'This is a catastrophe. Our guests aren't going to like this at all.'

'Yes, sir. But I'm sure if Rose Johns could voice an opinion, she would rather not have been killed.'

'Of course. I'm sorry. How do you want to do this?'

'Are most of your guests in the building now?'

'Yes, I'm fairly sure they are all in the dining room having their lunch.'

Matt glanced at Rick, who acknowledged his tactics had been on the mark. 'Perhaps,' he said to Neil, 'we should catch them at the end of the meal. You could introduce us and then I'll let them know this is now a murder investigation and that I'll need to see all of them individually – even those few we've already seen.'

'Please, Inspector, you will remember they're old and some, like Alice Littleton, for example, veer towards a naturally nervous disposition.'

'Mr Carstairs, I have had some experience in interviewing witnesses.'

'Yes, of course.' Flustered, Neil glanced at his watch. 'There is a bit of time before they finish. If you don't mind, I'd like to find Sonja – have her on stand-by in case anyone gets seriously upset?'

'That's fine. We'll wait here.'

'Thanks.' Neil hurried out to find Sonja, his assistant director, as well as Blue Moon's medical expert.

Rick looked sideways at Matt. 'Of course, for the very nervous we could tell them you're Esme's Matt. That should reassure them!'

'Can it. And I thought I said it wasn't to be mentioned again.'

'I know you said that, but you can't expect me to keep it quiet. It's pure gold!'

Matt sighed. He may have hoped but in all seriousness had not really expected Rick to let it go. Also, if he was honest, were the tables reversed, there was no way he would have kept it under wraps.

Neil returned with Sonja and the four made their way to the dining room. Practically the first person Matt saw was Esme, who was chattering happily to her table companions, Celia and Lucy, as she drank her coffee. He observed Celia notice the new arrivals and quickly bring him to Esme's attention, who turned in her chair and, seeing him, waved with a big smile.

He groaned.

Rick laughed and sent Esme a wave in return.

'Don't encourage her!' Matt muttered as the two made their way to her table. Fortunately, she excused herself from Celia and Lucy and stood to meet them.

'What are you doing here today?' Matt frowned.

'Working.' Esme gave a disarming smile that failed to disarm.

'But this isn't one of your regular days for Blue Moon.'

'It is sometimes when the workload is high.'

'And it's high today?' Matt was sceptical.

'Yes. Lots to sort out.' She gave Matt an innocent look that did not deceive him for a millisecond. 'I thought I could lend a hand. Make workloads lighter. Many hands make—'

Matt interrupted her rambling. 'I don't want you to get involved with this.'

'Wouldn't dream of it.' Seeing Matt's expression, she quickly looked past him. 'Hi, Rick.'

Amused, Rick answered, 'Hi. Great to see you here. Perhaps,' he lowered his voice, 'you can pick up some inside information for us?'

Matt snorted. 'I mean it, Esme. Keep out of this.'

'Of course.' She smiled at Rick as he turned to follow Matt back to Neil's side before returning to her table.

At this point Neil summoned everyone's attention. 'As some of you know, these gentlemen are Detective Inspector Devlin and Detective Sergeant Preston. They are here to investigate Rose's death.' He looked at Matt, who responded to his cue.

'As Mr Carstairs says, we are here looking into Rose John's death. Initially, it was thought to be an accident, but we now know that she was deliberately killed.'

There was a gasp round the room.

'So our investigation is now one of murder. This means we will need to talk with all of you, one at a time. I hope you will all be willing to cooperate and we shall try to disrupt your lives as little as possible. Mr Carstairs has kindly offered us the use of his office and he will direct you in turn to see us over the course of today and tomorrow.'

Wally spoke up. 'I take it this means we are all suspects?'

Another shocked gasp followed by murmurings throughout the room.

'Technically, yes. But we'll do our best to sort this matter out as soon as we can.' Matt waited a few seconds, but with no further comments forthcoming, he nodded at Neil, then left the dining room with Rick.

They had not been in the office long before Neil arrived, accompanied by a tall, spare man wearing old-fashioned horn-rimmed spectacles and a surprisingly lush head of hair.

'This is Peter Francis,' Neil said before withdrawing and closing the door.

Matt gestured towards the chair facing the desk. 'Thank you for agreeing to see us. I understand you were waiting for us all morning. I'm sorry for the delay. I hope it didn't put you out too much.'

Peter sat down, clearly more relaxed than when he first entered. Matt's greeting having had the desired effect. 'No problem. Only too pleased to help. Awful business, particularly as you now say she was killed.'

'Just so.' Matt checked that Rick was ready to record the interview and take notes. 'Mr Francis, I understand you came downstairs on Wednesday night. Would you tell us exactly what happened?'

'I was in bed but still awake. I'm afraid I don't sleep well nowadays. Anyway, I heard footsteps running past my door. I wondered what the rush was. Not often you hear that here. Shortly afterwards I heard someone running in the opposite direction. I was intrigued, so I put on my dressing gown and opened my door to see Lucy walking past. I asked her what was going on. She told me Rose had fallen down the stairs and was dead and that she'd been sent by Celia to fetch Sonja. So I accompanied Lucy down to the hall.'

After a pause Matt prompted, 'And then?'

'Oh, I thought the rest would have been covered by Celia and Lucy.'

'We'd like to hear your version of what happened.'

'Okay. We went downstairs and Rose was on the floor with a throw covering her. I stepped round her and went over to Celia. She said Sonja was calling for the doctor as Rose was not dead. Then Celia took Lucy back upstairs. She, Lucy, can be a little highly strung and I think Celia wanted her away from the scene. Then Celia returned and Sonja came out of the office saying the doctor was on his way. There seemed to be no point in hanging around, so I went back to my room.'

'Did you see anything untoward? Anything out of place? Anybody either upstairs or in the hall apart from the three women already mentioned?'

'Apart from Rose, I can't think of anything that struck me as strange.' He closed his eyes in thought for a few moments before saying more firmly, 'No, nothing seemed out of place. As for people, I definitely only saw Lucy, Celia and Sonja.'

'What did you think of Rose Johns?'

Peter hesitated. 'I didn't like her.'

'And your reasons?'

'She was like a cat among the pigeons. She seemed to upset most, if not all, of us. And I include the staff.'

'How did she upset you?'

'Me? I didn't like the way she upset Alice.' At Matt's raised eyebrow he elucidated. 'Alice Littleton. She's a gentle soul and chairs the Residents' Association's meetings.' He paused, quirking his head to one side.

'I know about the Residents' Association,' Matt confirmed.

'Well, you'll know then that it's an informal group. It's worked well all the time I've been here – five years now. Anyhow, Rose came along to a couple of meetings, saying there should be proper minutes and so on. It upset Alice, then Rose went on to imply that as Alice had not been formally elected as chair, that the whole set-up was undemocratic. Alice was so agitated she came straight to the office here to resign. Luckily, Neil and your Esme dissuaded her.'

Heroically disregarding Rick's grin, Matt said to Peter, 'Thank you, Mr Francis. I think that's all for now.'

Peter stood, then paused. 'I didn't like Rose, in fact I'd be surprised if anyone here did, but I don't like the idea of a killer among us. I hope you find him soon, Inspector.' He left the room.

The next interviewee was Sonja. She appeared calm as she came in and sat down. Before Matt could open the proceedings she spoke. 'I'm sorry I wasn't available yesterday when you wanted to see me. I'd been up most of the night and, of course, it was so upsetting. I was totally drained and Hugh – that is, Dr Saunders – insisted I go to bed.'

'That's perfectly all right. Now, we would like you to tell us about Wednesday night.'

This she did concisely and calmly, only becoming a little agitated as she recounted the doctor finding Rose Johns dead. Matt put this down to her nursing skills not meeting requirements – she had not realised Rose had died since her first examination and a feeling of guilt that she could in some way have taken action to prevent it.

'Just to clarify, Mrs Davies, the only time you were alone with Rose Johns was after Miss Foster had retired and before the doctor arrived?'

She thought a moment before replying, 'Yes, I think so. Of course, there was also a short time when Dr Saunders phoned for an ambulance and yourselves.'

'But by then Rose Johns was known to be dead?'

'Yes, of course.'

'What did you think of the deceased?'

Sonja pursed her lips. 'I didn't like her, to be honest. She was a troublemaker and a vindictive woman. Before all this happened I was intending to confer with Neil to see if there wasn't some loophole we could exploit so we could give her notice to leave.'

Matt nodded. 'Thank you, Mrs Davies. We will probably need to speak with you again.'

'Any time, Inspector.' She quietly left the office.

Matt looked at Rick. 'Both of them seem to have been honest – certainly in their opinions of Rose.'

'Yup. Looks more and more unlikely we're going to find a fan. She seems to have been a real bitch.'

Matt nodded. 'But she's still our murder victim. We'd better see if the Misses Strong and Foster can spare us a few minutes.'

The two women were found and seen individually. They

both went over and confirmed their previous statements. When asked what they thought of the murdered woman, they received the replies they had expected.

Lucy said, 'I didn't like her at all. She was horrid – like an evil worm in our Blue Moon apple.'

Celia said, 'She was a dreadful woman, picking on the weaker members of our little community here. And, although I've no hard proof, I'm pretty sure she was a blackmailer.'

Matt was startled. No one had mentioned this before. 'Who was she blackmailing?'

'I'd rather not go into specifics – no proof, as I said. Just a strong feeling from some observations. I could, of course, be quite wrong.'

Despite further pressing Celia refused to say more. When she had left the office the two men sat in contemplation until Matt shifted in his seat.

'It's getting on now, I think we'll leave further questioning until tomorrow.'

'Suits me.' Rick put away his notebook and pen. 'I'll get these transcribed first thing in the morning.'

'Good man.' They tracked down Neil and arranged matters for the following day, then left.

❧

As Matt had expected, Esme was waiting to pounce on him that evening for news on the progress of his investigation.

'You know I'm not supposed to talk with you about ongoing cases. Especially when you're involved, even in a peripheral way.'

'Oh pooh. No one has to know – and I might be able to help.'

'You're not to interfere. And you're certainly not to do any investigating yourself.'

'I wasn't going to start interrogating people for goodness' sake. Just sort of keep my eyes open and ears flapping.'

'Esme, I mean it. I know you like everyone at Blue Moon, but you mustn't forget that one of them is a cold-blooded murderer. He or she killed an unconscious woman.'

'I know, but—'

'Esme! No. However nice they seem, if the killer thinks you know too much, they could easily turn on you.'

She pondered on this for a while as she served their suppers. Matt hoped the realisation of the threat of putting herself in danger would curb her enthusiasm for sleuthing.

'Matt, I just can't see any one of them killing me.'

He groaned. 'Don't forget the first kill is the hard one. After that it becomes easier. I just don't want you in danger. Remember what happened at Holtexim.' In a previous case, involving murder and smuggling at the company where Esme had worked, there had been several attempts to kill her before she unearthed incriminating evidence through her work.

This remembrance did seem to have an impact on her and for some time they ate in silence. Finally, Matt unbent slightly. 'As I said, I can't discuss the case with you, but there's no reason you shouldn't talk about it to me.'

She eyed him askance. 'In other words, I can help you but you won't tell me anything.'

'Yup.'

'You don't think that's a bit one-sided?'

He sighed. 'Never mind then. We'll just keep to other subjects.'

'No.' It was her turn to give in. 'Obviously there's something you want to know. What is it?'

Matt asked a few generic questions. He wanted to lead up to the blackmail thread gently. Finally, he switched to motives. 'Motive is a bit of a stumper. I mean, I know she was generally disliked, that she upset several people, seemingly on purpose. But enough to kill her?'

'You never met her alive. She was a real witch.'

'Still, usually motives are centred on greed, passion, fear, blackmail, self-defence and so on. Not dislike.'

'I think in some cases it was more than dislike. Hate is not too strong a word.'

'Who do you think hated her?'

Esme regarded him thoughtfully for a moment. 'Do you know, I think you're right. We shouldn't discuss your work, especially an ongoing investigation.'

'Touché.' Matt saluted her with his glass of water. The conversation picked up shortly as they talked about their planned outing to meet their friends, Marcia and Peter Franks, on Sunday.

CHAPTER EIGHT

The next morning, Saturday, Matt intended to finish the preliminary interviews with the Blue Moon residents and staff, while Esme planned on a little housework before getting on with some bookkeeping for another of her clients. Esme's mobile rang as they were finishing breakfast. She looked at the display.

'Oh, it's Neil.'

Matt chewed the last piece of toast as he listened with growing resignation. Sure enough, as she disconnected the phone she smiled at him brightly.

'Neil says that Rose's nephew is coming to Blue Moon later this morning to collect her belongings and sort out the admin. He asked if I could go in to deal with settling Rose's accounts. Of course, I agreed.'

'Of course.' Matt carried his plate and empty coffee mug over to the sink.

'I could hardly say no.'

'Even if you'd wanted to.'

'Matt! Be reasonable.'

'I'd just rather you spent as little time there as possible until we've cleared matters up and identified the killer.'

'I'll be fine.' She smiled cheekily. 'Most of them like me.'

'I'm sure they do – including our killer. But if he feels under threat of exposure from you, I don't think "liking" is going to carry much weight.'

'I'll be careful. You know me.' She ignored his snort. 'Anyway, I'll be in the office most of the time dealing with the nephew.'

Matt kissed the top of her head as he passed. 'Just take care.' At the door he paused. 'What time is the nephew expected?'

'Around eleven, I think.'

'I'll ring Carstairs, let him know I want a look round her room again before everything's packed up.'

'Some clearing up may have already been started.'

'Well, I'll ask him to stop any more being done.' He pulled out his phone as he went to collect his jacket.

Matt and Rick arrived at Blue Moon to be met by Paula. 'Neil told me your message. I'm afraid we already did some clearing up yesterday. We thought as you and your team had already looked round in the room, you had finished with it.'

'Don't worry about it, Mrs Carstairs. I'd just like another quick look through her belongings.'

'We've put her things together but not packed them as we're not sure of her nephew's wishes. Of course we've stripped the bed and removed the towels and mats.'

She was clearly dismayed. Matt continued to soothe her as he and Rick made for the stairs, so that she had calmed down by the time they reached Rose's door. She remained just inside the room as the two men began to go through the possessions neatly laid out on the bed.

'Are you aware of anything missing, Mrs Carstairs?'

'No. Not that I might know if something was. Sonja

may have a better idea – she spent a lot of time in here while nursing Rose. Also, your Esme, she was a real godsend in giving Sonja some respite. I'm afraid Rose was not a particularly good patient.'

'So I understand.'

Matt and Rick finished their inspection, thanked Paula and retired downstairs to the office where they found Neil and a recently arrived Esme. She smiled at the two men as Neil put forward his request.

'I know you have more interviews to do. However, when Rose's nephew, Colin Bucknell, arrives, we will need the office to sort everything out. I don't know where to put you.'

'I understand he's expected about eleven?'

Neil nodded.

'We could perhaps start with some of your staff. The ones who don't live in.'

'Surely they're not under suspicion? They weren't here, as you said.'

'They're not suspected of anything. However, they did interact with Rose Johns, as well as with other people here.'

'Oh, I see.'

'Perhaps we could see them one at a time in the dining room? I presume it's empty at the moment?'

'Yes. That would be fine.' He hesitated.

'Is there a problem, Mr Carstairs?'

'Not exactly, just… I'd be grateful if you didn't upset them. They have already been through a stressful time, particularly Marj Simms and Jan Banks.'

'Don't worry. I'll make it crystal clear they're not under suspicion, that I just want to ask some questions to understand how Rose Johns fitted in here.'

'That's good, thank you. If you like to follow me, I'll

set you up in the dining room and fetch them. Is there any particular order in which you'd like to see them?'

As it turned out they started with Maria White. She asked to go first as she needed to be back in the kitchen to prepare lunch.

'You are the cook?' Matt clarified.

'Yes. I am a good cook.'

'I'm sure you are,' Matt agreed.

'It is not just me who says so,' Maria went on. 'Many of the people says it to me, or to Marj.' She paused. 'It is only that woman who complains.'

'You mean Rose Johns?'

'Yes. Absolutamente. She makes big fuss. Wants a special menu. How I am suppose to do that by myself? Eh?'

Matt assumed no reply was required. He was right, Maria continued, 'Mrs Paula, she help. She cook for that woman.'

Judging that the cook could not help their investigation any further, Matt thanked her for her time and asked if she would send in Jan Banks.

The cleaner turned out to be small and dark-haired. She entered and sat down in front of Matt. Her hands folded neatly in her lap, she looked at him enquiringly.

Matt smiled. 'Mrs Jan Banks?'

'Yes.'

'I understand you had some dealings with Rose Johns?'

Her expression darkened. 'I did. She complained about my work to Mr Neil. Said my "standards" were very low. No one else has ever had any complaints.'

'I believe she could be quite a difficult person,' Matt murmured.

'Difficult? Impossible, if you ask me. I was going to give my notice but Mrs Paula begged me not to.'

'Mrs Carstairs clearly values your work,' Matt mollified her. 'What I wanted to ask was if you'd noticed anyone going in or out of her room? Someone with no apparent legitimate reason.'

Jan shook her head.

'Or even someone showing an unusual interest?'

'No. No one.'

'Did you help Mrs Carstairs to collect together Mrs Johns' personal possessions yesterday?'

'Yes, ready for her nephew who's coming today.'

Matt nodded. 'Was everything there, as far as you know? Did you notice anything missing?'

'No, I don't think so. Is something missing then?'

'Probably not. I asked because as you regularly cleaned her room, you would have a good idea of what she possessed.'

'I certainly didn't take anything.'

'No. There is no suggestion of that.' After a few more general questions, Matt let her go.

While they waited for the waitress to appear, Rick asked, 'What's your thinking about the room and if anyone showed undue interest in it? She seems to have been a bitch and pushed someone too far.'

'Possible – even probable. But we mustn't lose sight that there could be other motives. She was a wealthy woman and not everyone here is.'

'You think someone knew of her fall, robbed then killed her – all on the spur of the moment?' Rick was sceptical.

'We don't know for sure that her fall was accidental.'

'You mean she was pushed, robbed, then killed to cover it up?'

'I'm not saying that's what happened. Just that there are other possibilities that shouldn't be ruled out yet.'

The door opened and a bright face peered in at them. 'Do you want to see me now?'

'Marjorie Simms? Yes, please come in and sit down.'

This she did while saying, 'Call me Marj, everyone does. Neil says I'm not a suspect.'

'He's right, you're not. But you knew Rose Johns and, of course, you know all the other residents.'

'Well, I only had dealings with Mrs Johns when I served at mealtimes. She wasn't a bit friendly like the others.'

Matt was regaled with the complaints of the menu, the quality of the food. The problems this caused in the kitchen. Jan's cleaning and near resignation. 'You just would not believe that one person could cause so much trouble. And, of course, that's not even mentioning all the upsets she caused among the guests.' She sat back, no doubt trying to catch her breath.

'Is there any guest in particular she upset?'

Marj's eyes unfocussed while she thought. 'I can't think of anyone in particular. To be honest, she seemed to upset everyone she spoke to!'

After a few general enquiries, Matt thanked her.

'Do you know how long you're going to be here? I need to start laying the tables for lunch soon.'

'That's okay. We'll be off now. Perhaps you could let Mr Carstairs know we'll be back around two?'

'Sure thing.' Marj smiled at both detectives before setting off to deliver the message.

'We'd better not be here when she gets back, come on.' Matt and Rick left to find their own lunch and to contact Dr Hugh Saunders to fix a time to meet him, preferably later in the afternoon.

Meanwhile, Colin Bucknell, Rose's nephew, had arrived. Esme studied him as Neil ushered him into the office and introduced them to each other. She judged he was a middle-management type and, given his age – late fifties – unlikely to rise any further. In some respects she could see some similarities with Jerry Hunt, the office manager at her last place of employment.

'We're sorry for your loss,' Neil said, although Bucknell did not look precisely sad. More irritated, perhaps.

'I wanted to make arrangements for my aunt's body to be picked up, but the undertaker informed me that it can't be released at the moment. Do you know what the cause of the delay is?'

'I imagine because of the post-mortem,' Neil said quietly.

'It can't be that complicated, surely, just an accident.'

Neil closed his eyes a second, then said, 'I'm sorry, Mr Bucknell, when I notified you of your aunt's death, I was under the impression it was an accidental fall down the stairs that had been the cause. Unfortunately, the police have found that she was murdered.'

'Murdered! What, you mean someone deliberately threw her down the stairs?'

'I'm not clear on the finer details. The police have not been very forthcoming.'

'This is insupportable. You charge high enough fees, how could you let this happen?'

'I don't see how I could have foreseen—'

'Nonsense. You vet prospective residents surely. Or maybe it was one of your staff – they should have their credentials checked before allowing them to work here.'

'Mr Bucknell, I appreciate this has been a shock to you – as indeed it was to us. However,' he brushed aside an attempted interruption, 'there is nothing any of us can do until the police find the culprit.'

There was a charged silence until Esme broke in. 'Mr Bucknell, perhaps we should get on with the financial aspect?'

Giving Neil a final glare, he turned to her. 'Fine. By all means.'

Neil took the opportunity to leave, muttering something about tracking down his wife.

Once the paperwork was finished, Esme explained that Mrs Carstairs would be taking him upstairs to Rose's room where her possessions were ready for him. As if on cue, the door opened to admit Paula. She shook his hand.

'I'm so sorry about your aunt.'

'Yes. Yes. Let's get on with it, then.'

Giving Esme a speaking look, Paula led the way out.

કર્જ

As arranged, Matt and Rick returned to Blue Moon, where they were able to re-commandeer the office. Their first interviewee was Alice. It was immediately apparent to both of the detectives that she was positively quivering with nerves as she sat on the edge of the chair. Matt, in an attempt to relax her, asked some questions about the length of time she had lived in Blue Moon, what she thought of it and even mentioned that Esme had told him of her sterling work for the Residents' Association. Rick grinned at this blatant use of Esme's popularity and her connection with Matt. However, it was this last tactic that produced a smile and some easing of her painfully tense posture. Only then could he begin the interview proper.

'Mrs Littleton, could you tell us your views of Rose Johns?'

'Rose... such a dreadful thing to happen. Do you think she suffered?'

'I've been assured it is very unlikely. But how did you see her?'

Alice looked torn. 'Of course, she hadn't been here long. I expect she was finding it difficult to adjust.'

'You may be right. The thing is, I'm trying to build an accurate picture of Mrs Johns and to do that I need everyone to give me their personal impression of her. What did you think of her?'

After a pause, Alice said softly, 'I didn't like her. And I don't think she liked me.'

'Who do you think did like her?'

'Truly, I'm not sure anyone did. She could be... sharp with people. With me, she seemed to find me incompetent, especially in relation to the Residents' Association. It was most distressing. I wanted to resign but Neil and your Esme persuaded me to continue.' She smiled. 'They were very persuasive.'

Matt smiled in return before returning to business. 'On the night Rose fell down the stairs, did you hear anything? Thuds? Voices? People moving about?'

She shook her head. 'No. Nothing at all. I slept through everything, even the ambulance and police arriving. I generally do sleep deeply, although not so well since she died.'

'That's understandable.'

'No, you don't understand. I feel so guilty...' She broke off.

'Guilty? About what? You weren't there.'

'No, but I wished her gone. Oh, not dead, just that she'd leave and things could go back to normal. As they were before she arrived. Peter said she obviously didn't like it here and so she might leave. That's what I wished for.'

'I see. But there's no reason for you to feel guilty. Wishing someone would go away is not a crime.'

'No, of course not. I'm just being silly. Take no notice.'

Matt thanked her while Rick held the door open for her relieved departure.

'A bit of a nervous Nora,' Rick observed.

'I imagine she'd been wishing Rose dead and then suddenly she was. It's not uncommon for people in that situation to start to think that their wishing had been part of the cause.' He shrugged. 'Anyway, we'd better get a move on.'

Jane Masters was the next to be seen. A smart widow, a confident woman. She freely admitted to not liking Rose. When pressed for a reason, she just said Rose was unpleasant and the root of the dismal atmosphere settling over Blue Moon. And no, she had had no personal altercation with the dead woman. She went on to say no, she had heard nothing on Wednesday night. The first she knew anything about it was at breakfast the following morning.

Penny Childs was the next to be heard.

'No, I didn't like her. Rather an unpleasant person. I did think at one time, while on a walk, that she wanted to be friendly with me. But there was just a feeling that something wasn't right and then Larry came over and seemed annoyed with her and took me off.'

She also had not heard nor seen anything on the night in question.

Bob Pargeter, the next interviewee, came across as a man who clearly lived in the present. He was comfortably off and with no close family left, just a slew of relatives waiting to inherit. For that reason he felt justified in freely spending his money. Matt admired his candour but again he had nothing to aid their investigation.

The following two to be seen individually were Oswald (Wally) Abbott and Albert (Al) West. Both had enjoyed very successful high-flying careers and were apt to keep to each other's company, as they quite clearly understood each other. Neither were interested in gossip or meaningless chitter-chatter. Neither had anything to help the investigation apart from sharing a meal with Rose once and not particularly liking her. 'Troublemaker', according to Wally. 'A wrong 'un', according to his friend.

Charles Green came across as a loner. But a loner who observed and analysed the behaviour of others. His testimony was of value only in fleshing out the characters of those in Blue Moon and confirming some of their statements. He also had not liked Rose as she had disrupted the peace and contentment he had relished.

Larry Dunns was the last to be admitted to the office. After the preliminaries were over, when he was asked for his views on Rose, he was frank.

'Penny Childs, as you probably know, has her place here paid for by the local authority. All well and good, but it doesn't cover those little extras that make life more enjoyable. I admit I was drawn to her from the beginning and, well, I've more than enough of the green stuff, so I made a private arrangement with Neil. She, Penny, was not to know about it. No one was, apart from your Esme as she does all the bookkeeping here. I have no idea how, but Rose found out about it and decided to hold it over me. Honestly, I was livid. Both Neil and Esme denied telling anyone, and I believe them. I mean, why start blabbing now and to such a woman? Besides, once my initial anger settled a bit, I remembered I trust them without any reservation. So I sorted Rose out myself.'

'How?' Matt asked mildly.

Larry gave a rueful grin. 'Not by killing her! No, I made some enquiries, found some dirt on her and promised I'd fight fire with fire. She backed off straight away.'

'Would you care to let us know the, er, "dirt" you dug up?'

'No. It has no bearing on your investigation. No one else here knew anything about it. And the woman is dead now.'

Matt let it go for the time being. If later on he thought the information pertinent, he would get it out of Dunns, regardless of his ethics.

Once Dunns had left the office, he looked at his partner. 'When are we seeing Dr Saunders?'

'It's been rearranged for tomorrow, first thing, as he's going out for the day.'

Matt groaned. 'Sunday?'

'Well, I could contact him again and rearrange it for Monday?'

'Yes, see if he's agreeable. It's getting late now. I suggest after you've spoken to the good doctor, that we knock off. Tomorrow I'd like to get the incident board updated and prepare our reports for the SIO on Monday.'

'Great.' Rick set about phoning Dr Saunders to defer his interview to Monday.

❧

The following morning, Matt and Rick sorted out their interview notes and transferred relevant information on to the incident board, along with the names of all the suspects. SOCO had left a report saying they had identified the cushion used to asphyxiate the victim. Unfortunately, the chances of extracting and identifying DNA, other than Rose John's, would be a long shot. The cushion was not new and clearly had countless people's DNA on it. The two detectives then collaborated on the report to be presented to the SIO in the morning before leaving the station to salvage what was left of the weekend.

Early evening, Matt and Esme met up with Marcia and Peter at a small restaurant which sported wonderful views of the South Downs. The weather was balmy so they decided to sit outside. Peter and Matt had been friends since they were at school together. Esme had met Marcia when she went to work at the now-defunct Holtexim and they had soon become fast friends.

Conversation flowed generally until Marcia asked, 'So, how's business doing, Esme?'

'Really well. Much better than I could have hoped for. I mean, I was banking on some small businesses being interested in having their bookkeeping done for them, but I had no idea there were so many locally.'

'Yes, I remember you saying you were prepared to expand your customer base by looking further afield.'

'I've no need to do that, at least not at the moment. I've got plenty of work just now,' Esme said happily.

Peter smiled. 'You're lucky, it's often initially hard to get this sort of concern going.'

'Esme's really good at her job,' Matt said fondly. 'Once someone gives her a trial, that's it, they keep her on. In fact, the last two came to you from recommendations, didn't they?'

'Word of mouth. Best advertising ever. Well done, Esme,' Peter congratulated her.

She flushed with pleasure. 'Well, of course, it's early days yet.'

Marcia would not hear of this. 'You're a success, Esme. And you deserve it after all your hard work setting up your stall, so to speak.'

Peter took the pressure off Esme by addressing Matt. 'Any interesting cases you're working on?'

Matt grimaced. 'I suppose it'll all come out anyway. The latest involves the suspicious death of a woman at the Blue Moon old people's home—'

'Isn't that one of your clients, Esme?' Marcia broke in.

'Yes, they were my first.'

'So this is another murder you're involved in, Esme!' She sounded thrilled, then sobered. 'You're not going to be in any danger, are you?'

Matt answered. 'No, Esme is not involved really, solely as a peripheral although unfortunate connection. And, as long as she keeps out of it, there's no reason to think she's in any danger.'

Esme wrinkled her nose while Peter looked amused. Marcia, undaunted, continued, 'Do tell us all about it.'

Matt was firm. 'No, there really isn't much to say, anyway.' He looked at Peter. 'How's the architectural world doing?'

Still grinning, Peter accepted Matt's change of subject.

The rest of the evening passed pleasantly with only one jarring note for Matt as they said their goodbyes when he heard Marcia say sotto voce to Esme, 'You can tell me all about it another time. Really, you do seem to have more than your fair share of adventures!'

On the way home Matt said, 'I don't want you discussing this case with Marcia. For a start she's likely to want to "help" – a concept I find highly nerve-wracking.'

Esme laughed. 'Don't worry, Matt.' She patted his knee reassuringly.

It was not until much later, when Esme was asleep, that he realised she had not exactly answered him.

CHAPTER NINE

Early on Monday morning Matt and Rick visited Dr Hugh Saunders at his surgery before it opened for patients. He was a pleasant-looking man, rather than handsome, and Matt placed him in his late thirties.

'Thank you for agreeing to see us so early,' Matt said.

'Not at all. Freeing up Sunday meant I could meet up with some friends for a spot of fishing.'

He led the way to his consulting room. 'I presume this is about Rose Johns' death at Blue Moon?'

'That's right. I don't know if you've heard, but it's been established the fall didn't kill her. We're now treating her death as murder.'

'I see.' He sank into his chair. 'The actual cause?'

'Asphyxiation.' Matt watched him closely. 'Would you tell us your version of Wednesday night?'

Saunders surfaced from the little reverie he had fallen into at Matt's words. 'My version? Let's see, Sonja called me round about midnight. May have been slightly earlier. She said Rose Johns had fallen downstairs, broken some bones, but her main cause of concern was that she had not recovered consciousness. I said I'd come right away, which I did.' He paused for thought before continuing. 'When I arrived Sonja let me in.'

'Was anyone else there?'

'No, just Sonja. I know Mrs Johns was found by two of the residents but they had already gone to their rooms before I got there.'

'How would you describe the state Mrs Davies was in?'

'She was concerned, naturally, but composed. After all, she is a professional, fully trained nurse. And a damned fine one too. In some respects she's wasted at Blue Moon.'

Matt brought the doctor back to the point. 'What did you do then?'

'I went over to examine her, although the length of time she had been unconscious was obviously going to require a trip to the hospital.'

Matt broke in. 'Surely Mrs Davies would have recognised this? Why do you think she didn't call for an ambulance straight away?'

'It was very late, she had just been woken up…' He tailed off seeing Matt's raised eyebrow. He sighed. 'Sonja and I are good friends. I would like us to be more but she's hesitant. Has a peculiar hiccup over me being a few years younger. Still, we are particularly good friends and I can only think she immediately thought of me and then acted on it.'

Matt nodded. 'So, you looked at Mrs Johns?'

'Yes, I could see at a glance several bones had been broken – this, by the way, was why Sonja had covered her but not moved her, for fear of making an injury worse. I raised her eyelids, then checked for a pulse. There was none and she wasn't breathing.'

'You concluded she had died from the fall or shortly afterwards from shock?'

Saunders hesitated, then appeared to make up his mind. 'I was a bit concerned in that her lips appeared slightly blue and her eyes were bloodshot. However, not sufficiently to be sure of any additional cause of her death. Anyway, I knew a post-mortem would have to be carried out which would pin-point the actual cause of death. So my immediate concern was to report her death.'

'Then you...?' Matt prompted as the doctor fell silent.

'Then I told Sonja she was dead. She was upset, understandably so, both from the viewpoint of the woman being dead but also as she jumped to the conclusion that she had made a mistake when she had examined her. I told her Mrs Johns must have died after her examination. Once she was calmer I called for an ambulance and the police. After that I waited with Sonja until the services arrived. Carstairs had arrived by then, of course. The rest you know.'

'Thank you, Doctor, both for your time and candour.'

Saunders rose. 'I told all this to the policeman that night.'

'Just double-checking. And, of course, that night it was thought to be an accident.'

'Yes, I see.' He grew pensive. 'Now you're looking for a killer. Am I suspect? Is Sonja?'

'We have a duty to look at anyone who had opportunity.' Matt gave the usual non-committal reply, then unbent slightly. 'No one has been pin-pointed as yet. We have only narrowed the field to those in the building at the time. Now we have to look for motives – much harder!'

'Oh, I don't know. Rose Johns was not the most popular person there.'

'Agreed!' Matt turned at the door. 'Good luck with your pursuit of Sonja Davies.'

Saunders grinned. 'Oh, I've no intention of giving up.'

�❧�

Paula and Neil were having breakfast alone together, Selina not yet having risen from her bed. 'You should have something more than just coffee,' Paula fretted.

'Don't fuss. I'm not hungry, if I feel peckish later I'll fall on Maria's magnanimity.' He was skimming the newspaper. 'Nothing more about Rose's death, certainly no mention of murder. We must be grateful for small mercies, I suppose. Although really it's more of a delay. Perhaps it would be better to get it over with.'

'What do you mean?'

'Murder, here – it'll make the news at some time. Not going to be good for business.'

'No, I suppose not. Really, that woman is causing as much trouble dead as she did alive. And that's saying something.'

Neil smiled at her. 'I hardly think we can blame her for being killed.'

'I can. She brought it on herself with her nastiness to everyone. Do you really think it'll hurt Blue Moon? It might just be a point of interest soon forgotten.'

'Not likely. Once the police have found their man, a trial will follow. We'll have journalists trying to catch the residents for "an exclusive". They won't like it, some may even decide to leave.'

'Oh Neil, surely not. We're like an extended family here. Granted, Rose caused disruption, but she's gone now. We can all settle back and things can return to what they were.'

Neil leant back. 'Perhaps you're right. I certainly hope you are.' He looked at his watch. 'Where's Selina? She'll be late for work.'

Paula moved to the door. 'I'll go and rattle her up.'

'Honestly, that girl has no sense of responsibility,' he grumbled before swallowing the last of his coffee.

ॐॐ

On Monday morning, Sonja and Paula were in the office impatiently waiting for Esme to arrive, which in a rush she did. Looking at their faces she said, 'Before you say anything about the time, I wasn't late, but I seem to have been stopped by nearly everyone wanting "insider" police information.'

She deposited her handbag in a drawer, missing the exchange of guilty looks between the other two women. She clicked her computer to start its booting-up procedure and drew her in-tray closer to sort its contents. It was the silence that finally caught her attention. She looked up, saw their expressions and groaned. 'Not you two as well.'

Paula leant back. 'You can't really blame us. All of us are suspects in the eyes of the police. They question us but don't give a clue as to what they're thinking – even when asked! You are our only link to what's going on with them.'

Sonja put her tuppence worth in. 'If the position were reversed, I'm sure you would want to know the state of play. Or at least what's likely to happen.'

Esme gave a rueful smile. 'You're right. I admit it. But Matt won't tell me anything – not even in confidence. He doesn't want me to get involved in any way. In fact, he's pretty hipped that I have a connection with Blue Moon and an obligation to be here at all.'

'He doesn't say anything at all? Not even to reassure you that certain people are not on their radar?' Paula probed.

'Nope. In fact, it's jolly infuriating, not to say damn aggravating!' Her tone one of disgust.

'Well, if he doesn't, he doesn't. I'm sure you tried to get the low-down, so to speak.' Sonja was philosophical.

'Yes, I did,' Esme admitted. 'But he can imitate a sphynx when it comes to his work.'

They sat in gloomy silence for a while before Paula said, 'I'm mostly worried about Neil. He's becoming more and more on edge. Part of it is concern for how it will affect the business. I mean, will some of the guests become so nervous about a killer in their midst that they decide to leave?'

Sonja nodded in agreement. 'That would affect all of us.' Esme understood. Sonja's son was at university and, although he had a scholarship, there were other expenses such as accommodation, food and books to be covered. She did not want him to graduate loaded down with crippling debts and therefore needed her income as assistant director from Blue Moon to continue to provide him with an allowance. Also, of course, she lived on the premises so if the business went belly up she would not only lose her position and income but her home as well.

'I just wish the police would find the killer. Then maybe we could go back to where we were before that dreadful woman came here. I blame her for everything.'

'They will,' Esme assured her. 'Matt's really good at his job.' Seeing their smiles, she added, 'And that's not just me being biased. He's pretty young to be a detective inspector. Also, he's on a police fast-track scheme, so his superiors must think he's first-rate.'

Paula relented. 'You've convinced me! I must say he's

not at all aggressive or intimidating in his questioning. Even some of our timid rabbits have opened up to him.'

Esme decided not to explain that his method was very successful in extracting extra information without the witness being aware of it. Such insight might make them more nervous and reticent with him.

'Well.' Sonja rose to her feet. 'I must get on.'

'Yes,' Paula agreed. 'We'll leave you in peace, Esme.'

The two left Esme deep in contemplation. It occurred to her that she was perceived as an insider to both sides. Matt and Rick wanted her to report on any relevant observations of those in Blue Moon, while those people wanted to know the progress of the police investigation. How double-agent spies managed it, sometimes for years on end, she had no idea. Shrugging, she returned to her work.

❦

Matt and Rick were in the SIO's office giving their report for his daybook. Matt finished up, 'The cushion used to asphyxiate the victim has been identified by SOCO. They've sent it to Meadows for confirmation that the DNA found on it came from Rose Johns. Unfortunately, although there is quite a lot of other DNA on it, it's not practical in terms of identifying our killer. The cushion is not new and no doubt been handled by several in the suspect pool.'

'Pity,' Shute observed.

'Quite,' Matt agreed.

'So what are your thoughts? Any hunches?'

'Not really, sir. We're still at the phase where there are a number of questions needing to be investigated.'

'Like?' Shute asked.

'For instance, to a large degree the Misses Foster and

Strong alibi each other. Is this because they're telling the truth, or have they collaborated to produce their stories?'

'You say "to a degree". Not watertight alibis then?'

Rick answered, 'Miss Strong is well covered, but Miss Foster did spend periods of time alone with the victim. When Miss Strong went to fetch the nurse, for example. Also, while the nurse went to call the doctor.'

'Then,' Matt took up the report, 'there is Mrs Davies, the nurse. She was alone with the body until the doctor arrived.'

'Dr Saunders,' Rick continued. 'He was the first to declare her dead. Perhaps he did it?'

Frank Shute looked doubtful. 'Leaving aside his motive, you think he'd do it with the nurse looking on?'

'They are special friends. They could have been in it together,' Rick defended.

Matt broke in, 'It is within the bounds of possibility but unlikely. For the time being I think we can leave the doctor out of the mix.'

'Anyone else?' Shute asked.

'It would appear that our victim was not averse to blackmail. We know of at least one instance, but as the target managed to spike her guns by, as he put it, "fighting fire with fire", I'm pretty sure we can rule him out. However, Miss Foster also said she was sure Rose Johns was a blackmailer. So someone else may have thought to eliminate the threat permanently.'

'I see. You certainly seem to have a number of threads to consider. Keep me posted.'

'Yes, sir.' The two detectives left the SIO's office to return to their desks to sift through all the interviews once again, trying to find any inconsistency or clue they had missed.

That evening Esme studiously avoided any topic that could be linked to Blue Moon or the investigation. After much thought she had decided she was not equipped to be a "double agent". Matt followed her lead until they were washing up.

'No questions about the case?' he teased.

'No. When I got to Blue Moon this morning, I had to run the gamut of quite a number of residents, all wanting to know who you suspected and how your enquiries were going. Even, when I got to the office, Paula and Sonja were waiting to quiz me. Then I remembered Rick saying I could keep a look out for your investigation.'

'And so you've decided to keep out of it?'

'I decided to keep any information to myself whether I get it from you or from the people at Blue Moon. I'm not cut out to be a spy, Matt.'

'I see. I can understand what you're saying. However, you should tell me anything that pertains to our investigation.'

Esme giggled. '"Pertains to your investigation". Really, Matt, we're not in a court of law!'

'No, and that might have sounded a bit pedantic, but, Esme—'

'Matt. If I find any concrete evidence, of course I'll tell you. But I won't be passing on any impressions or gossip.'

He looked searchingly at her, then smiled. 'Fair enough.'

CHAPTER TEN

John Meadow's complete post-mortem report was on Matt's desk when he arrived the next morning. There was a post-it note saying "You owe me one" stuck to its cover. Matt laughed as he removed it and opened the report.

'It seems our Rose was pushed down the stairs, rather than falling. There are fingertip bruises on her sternum. And she was killed by vagal inhibition… apparently this means the vagus nerve in her neck was compressed while she was being smothered which caused her heart to stop. This is possibly why the doctor wasn't sure – the signs were not as clear as with total asphyxiation. She died when her heart stopped, before the asphyxiation could finish the job.' He read on – then continued, 'So, she was asphyxiated, but not immediately after the fall.' He looked across at Rick. 'At least an hour passed between the fall and the asphyxiation.'

'Why wait an hour?'

'Why indeed. I think the fall, or push, probably happened during an argument. The pusher then left the scene, probably went to their own room. Later, someone else decided to capitalise on the situation and finish her off.'

'So, two people were involved?'

'I think so, but completely independent of each other. Collusion seems unlikely given the time lapse between the two events.'

'Anything else that might help us in there?'

'Only confirmation the cushion sent to him by SOCO was definitely the murder weapon. And, as SOCO thought, any other traces found on it are inconclusive for identifying the killer.'

Rick added the information to the incident board and the two men studied it for a minute or so.

Rick reaffirmed, 'We're looking for two people. The first event, we're assuming was an accident or impulse during some sort of altercation. The second was deliberate but, of course, could also have been done on the spur of the moment, on impulse.'

Matt sighed. 'As we're going on the premise that the two events were caused by two different people, I think we have to assume that the second event could not have been planned in advance. I mean, how could anyone have known Rose would fall and be knocked unconscious?'

They reverted to staring glumly in silence at the board. Finally, Matt returned to his desk.

'Okay. Let's talk motives. Blackmail is an obvious one. We know Larry Dunns was one of her targets, but he dealt with it by turning the tables on her. If she tried to blackmail him, there is a strong chance there were others. We need to find out who.'

Rick had written blackmail under motives on the board, followed by a question mark.

'Then,' Matt continued, 'we have the people she radically upset. Was one sufficiently distressed or angry to kill her?' He thought a moment. 'Larry Dunns could fall into this category, although unlikely.'

While writing on the board, Rick mooted, 'There are the Misses Foster and Strong. Also, Alice Littleton and Peter Francis.' He stood back to survey the list.

'Right,' said Matt. 'And we mustn't forget the staff. Did Sonja Davies reach her limit of patience while nursing her? Then there's Mrs Carstairs, worried about the adverse effect Rose was having in general and the knock-on effect this was having on her husband.' He pondered on this. 'No, I think we can scratch her. She would have realised the risks of a murder on the business. The same reasoning applies to her husband.'

Removing her name from the board, Rick replaced it with Jan Banks. 'The cleaner was upset enough to consider resignation.'

'Good.'

'What about the cook?'

'I doubt it, she had little or no direct contact with Rose. And Mrs Carstairs had, in effect, removed the problem from her.'

'That just leaves Marj Simms.'

Matt smiled. 'Very unlikely. Not the temperament at all.'

'Right,' Rick agreed. 'We'll leave those two off.'

'But just for the time being.'

'What about the three men Green, Abbot and West?'

'From what we know so far, I can't see what motive they could have had.'

Rick agreed. 'I could look into their backgrounds to see if anything pops up.'

'Good idea. And I'll do the same with Francis and Sonja Davies.' The two detectives moved off to give their update to Frank Shute.

Meanwhile, at Blue Moon the talk was nearly all centred on Rose and her killer. Charles entered the communal lounge to wait for the summons to lunch. He saw Al and Wally, who waved him over.

'We've been trying to think who killed Rose,' Wally said.

'Isn't that the job of the police?' Charles asked mildly.

'Of course. But when we know it's someone here, someone we know… well, it makes you think.'

'Yes. Makes you think,' Al echoed.

'I suppose,' Charles conceded. 'Who are your main suspects then?'

'That's the problem,' Wally admitted. 'As soon as we consider anyone, we only seem to come up with reasons they couldn't have done it.'

'I can see your dilemma.' Charles half-smiled.

'So who do you think it could be?' Wally pushed.

'Me? I've no idea.' He cogitated while the other two watched him expectantly. 'I understand she was smothered?'

The other two nodded.

'That makes it much harder to narrow down.' Seeing their expressions, he elucidated. 'It could have been a woman as easily as a man. Not much strength needed to hold a pillow over an unconscious person's face.'

Wally and Al looked at each other. Wally said, 'We weren't even considering the women.'

'No.' Al looked glum. 'Makes our pool even bigger.'

Just then, Marj poked her head round the door. 'Ah, there you are. Lunch is ready,' she informed them, and quickly disappeared.

At their table for two, Alice leant towards Peter. 'I can't

help wondering when I see one of the others, are they the one?'

'Even me?'

'Don't be silly. But you must admit it's creepy not knowing if you're talking to a killer.'

'Alice, you mustn't let it get into your head. The police will sort it out.'

She relaxed slightly. 'Yes, you're right. Esme's Matt will get to the bottom of it.'

'Yes.' A pause, then, 'A pity, really.'

'A pity? Why?'

'As you say, it'll be someone we know and like.'

'Yes.' She forked a mouthful of Maria's inimitable macaroni cheese into her mouth while she mused on the quandary.

At another table, Lucy desultorily pushed some pasta round her plate.

Celia finally asked tartly, 'Are you going to eat that or just play with it?'

Lucy laid her fork down. 'Celia, let's leave here. Today. We could go to a hotel while we look for something more permanent.'

Celia stared at her, astounded. 'Where did this come from?'

'Someone here killed Rose.'

'I know. We've known it virtually from the start. What's got you in such a tizzy now?'

'Celia, they could kill again!'

'I doubt it. Rose upset everyone, that's why she was killed. There's no reason for anyone else to be killed.'

'I suppose so,' Lucy agreed in an ambivalent tone.

'In any case, I'm pretty sure we'd not be allowed to go until the police have finished their enquiries.'

'Oh goodness. You don't think we're under suspicion – you and I?'

'If television police programmes are to be believed, I imagine everyone is suspected. Of course, some may be more suspected than others.'

'And us?'

Celia relented. 'I can't see why we should have anything to worry about.'

'Well, we did find Rose. That could be seen as suspicious.'

'Rose wasn't dead then. Sonja said so.'

'Yes, she did.' Bolstered by this reassuring thought, Lucy picked up her fork and took a hefty mouthful.

CHAPTER ELEVEN

'So,' Matt leaned back from his desk as he eyed his partner, 'did you turn up anything useful on Abbott, Green or Wood?'

'Not really. Green worked for a plumbing fittings manufacturer. Joined at twenty-three and spent the rest of his entire working life there.'

'Unusual.'

'Yes. Anyway, he worked on the distribution side in their central warehouse. Apparently a very reliable employee, he rose to be assistant manager and retired with a healthy pension and a chunk of company stock he had purchased over the years. He always seems to have been a natural loner.'

'Ever married?'

'Yes, for over thirty years. She died several years before he retired. No children. In fact, no immediate or close family. Some remote cousins, but they don't seem to keep in touch.'

'Rather sad.'

'You'd think so, but most of the people I spoke

to said that was how he liked it. And he wasn't one for joining groups. To the contrary, his living at Blue Moon is probably the most social time of his life. And even there he is considered by both staff and fellow residents as a loner.'

'Nothing much there to point to him as either the pusher-downstairs or smotherer.'

'Do you want his name on the board moved to the "Not possible" list?'

Matt thought. 'No. Leave him where he is at the moment. We've got nothing to completely rule him out.'

'Right. Then there's Oswald Abbott, invariably called Wally, and Albert West, known as Al. In the main they seem to keep to each other's company, probably because they have very similar backgrounds and therefore understand each other. They both had very successful high-flying careers – most of which they spent as directors or chief executives of several household-name companies. They had crossed paths during their careers but only really became friends when they both hove to at the Blue Moon. I gather they play chess, go for long tramps in the woods and are fairly regular patrons at the Dog & Duck. Neither are prone to waste words. In fact, taciturn was used to describe them.'

'So they're pretty much outsiders too?'

'Yes, but not so much as Green. Abbott and West seem to be quite popular amongst the others. Considered to be amusing – when something happens they can produce a dry comment which dispels any tension. Also, they're kind, even to those they don't take to.'

Matt looked quizzical.

'For instance, Rose Johns joined their table for a meal with neither making any demur. I also understand that after one of those residents' meetings when Rose had laid into Alice Littleton, both Al and Wally stood up for her.'

'I see. Again, not really the sort to go about killing people.'

'Not really. Shall I leave them on the "Possible" list?'

'Yes. For the time being at least.' Matt shuffled some papers. 'As for Peter Francis, he didn't have a great education. Left school with no certificates. Worked on building sites where he obviously picked up various skills as, when he retired, he was a deputy site manager. He worked for various companies but interestingly was never out of work. He has a pension, but it's small. He doesn't pay for his residency at Blue Moon, the local authority does. He's careful with his pension to ensure it stretches to cover some of the extras. He supports Alice Littleton as Deputy Chair of the Residents' Association – mainly, the general consensus believes, because he's sweet on her.'

'Sweet on her? How old are you, partner?' Rick teased.

'Just reporting what I was told! Anyway, he'll have to remain a possible – no alibi.'

'Do you think he was being blackmailed?'

Matt considered this. 'No, I don't think so. I haven't found anything worthy of blackmail material connected to him. It's no secret about his past or his financial situation.'

'What about the nurse?'

'Sonja Davies is forty years old and joined Blue Moon when Neil set it up. She's a fully accredited nurse and is responsible for all health concerns. After a couple of years, Neil Carstairs offered her the position of assistant director where, instead of salary, she receives a percentage of the profits. This, of course, makes it very unlikely she would do anything that could adversely affect the business. Especially as she would lose her home as well as income if it collapsed.'

Rick nodded.

'Divorced when she was twenty-nine. She has daughter, Mary Brent, of twenty-one who is expecting her first child. There's also a son, Fred, of nineteen. He's at university.'

'It seems unlikely she'd smother Rose Johns, but it can't be denied that she had the opportunity.'

'Yes, she'll have to be left under the possibles.'

They gazed gloomily at the board.

'We've not made much headway in eliminating suspects.'

'No,' Matt agreed. 'I think we should start looking at their alibis.'

❧

Esme had only just sat down at her desk when Paula came in, followed by Sonja. Both were laden with large cardboard boxes which they deposited against the wall with grunts of relief.

'Morning, Esme.'

'Morning.' She gestured to the boxes. 'What's in those?'

Paula explained. 'We've been clearing out all Rose's stuff. Her nephew didn't take much, just her jewellery and radio/CD player. Those,' she indicated the boxes, 'contain her books, photos, knick-knacks and shoes. Plus, there's a huge suitcase upstairs full of her clothes.'

'You just don't realise until you have to pack it all up, quite how much stuff people bring with them.' Sonja sank onto a chair. 'And she'd only been here a matter of weeks. Imagine what some of our long-stayers have accumulated!'

Paula agreed as she, too, sat down. 'I'm taking it all down to the charity shop in the village this afternoon. Although it looks as if I'll have to make two trips.'

'I don't mind taking some of it,' Esme offered.

Paula smiled at her. 'Thanks, Esme, that would be a great help.'

'No problem.' She pulled her in-tray closer.

'How're the police getting on with their investigation?'

Esme firmed her lips and dropped the few papers she was holding. 'I've done a lot of thinking about it and I told Matt that I wasn't going to be an informer on what's going on here – unless, naturally, it's hard evidence.' She eyed the two women facing her. 'And that goes both ways, I'm not passing on anything I learn from Matt.'

There was a stark silence, eventually broken by Paula's sigh. 'I understand. It has put you in rather an invidious situation.'

'Oh, I'm so glad you agree,' Esme said with relief. 'I didn't want it to affect our friendship, but seriously, it was making me uncomfortable.'

'Of course it won't spoil our friendship,' Sonja assured her, but then added, 'It's a pity, though.'

All three laughed while Sonja got them each a mug of coffee from the carafe on top of the book shelving.

Sobering, Paula said, 'I am concerned, though, that they find the culprit soon. I'm afraid until they do the heavy pall over everyone here will remain as they all look at each other wondering if it is them. Neil's worried that some may even want to leave.'

'I'm not sure the police would like that,' Esme ventured. 'Although, I suppose so long as they remained in the immediate area it wouldn't be so bad.'

'"Wouldn't be so bad"? It would be catastrophic,' Paula contradicted.

'Yes.' Sonja shook her head. 'It would be very bad for Blue Moon.'

'Well,' Esme was determinably cheerful, 'no one's left yet. They've been here for years, most of them. I'm sure they'll be faithful and ride out the present unpleasantness. After all, apart from the killer, they all know they're innocent. Right?'

'Right,' echoed Sonja.

'I really hope you are right.' Paula finished her coffee and rose. 'I'd better get on.'

'Yes, so must I. Especially if I'm gallivanting about this afternoon helping to deliver Rose's stuff to the charity shop.' Esme resumed sorting her in-tray.

❧

Instead of meeting in his office, Frank Shute joined Matt and Rick in front of the incident board. Frank looked over it carefully.

'I see you've exonerated six. You're sure of all of them?'

Matt replied, 'Neil and Paula Carstairs would have understood the damage to their business. If they had wanted Rose out of the way, I'm sure Neil could have found a way – probationary period not working out. Something on those lines. Larry Dunns, by his own admission, was threatened by Rose but dealt with the problem on a "biter bit" premise. As for Marj Simms, Jan Banks and Maria White, none of them were on the premises. They all live out.'

'I notice Esme's name is missing…?'

Matt saw the twinkle in Frank's eye. 'Not a joking matter, sir. Trying my best to keep her out of it!'

'Fat chance,' Rick muttered.

Shute openly grinned at him before turning serious again. 'And the rest?'

Matt blew out a frustrated breath. 'Regards the push

down the stairs, any of them could have done it, except for Lucy and Celia as they were out when that happened. Their return time to Blue Moon has been corroborated by the taxi driver's log.'

Rick picked up the report. 'To some extent, the murder itself is a bit easier to narrow down. As we know she was alive when the nurse first came down, and that Rose was not alone after that – it would seem her killer must be either Celia, Sonja, Peter or the doctor.'

'You're not including Lucy Strong?' Shute enquired.

'Not unless Celia is protecting her. She was never alone with Rose. Added to which she's scared of her own shadow. A real rabbit of a woman.'

'Mmm.' Shute absorbed this. 'All right. What about Sonja Davies? Her motive?'

'The only thing we can think of,' Matt said, 'is that she disliked the atmosphere being caused by Rose, perhaps exacerbated by the time she had to spend with her when she was nursing her – could this have been the final straw? On the other hand, she, like the Carstairs, would not have wanted any scandal to be attached to Blue Moon. It's her livelihood and place of residence. Too much for her to lose.'

'So she's only on your list as she had opportunity?'

'That's about it, sir.'

'Celia Foster?'

'Not much motive. Rose had upset Lucy and Celia is very protective of her. However, she had opportunity, having spent some time alone with the unconscious Rose. As did Peter Francis but, again with him, not much motive.'

'So what are your next steps?'

Matt replied, 'We have a number of questions needing answers, such as why was Rose coming downstairs at that time of night? Where was she heading?'

Rick wrote it on the board and numbered it, one.

Matt continued, 'What was the murky incident in Rose's past? Why was Peter Francis awake? If awake, how did he not hear the fall? Why would he go downstairs? Was he shocked to learn Rose was still alive at that stage? Had he thought her already dead as he was the one to push her downstairs?'

He thought a moment, which allowed Rick to finish writing on the board.

'Then,' Matt resumed, 'there are the missing items from Rose's room. When I say "missing", it's because I would have expected to find them there. No money at all. No diary or journal – most people have a diary if only to keep abreast of future appointments. No letters – I checked with Neil Carstairs and she had received her share. It's unlikely she read then destroyed all of them.'

They stared at the list. Frank asked, 'Where are you planning to start?'

'Of those that spent time alone with the unconscious Rose, Celia and Sonja have logical reasons to be there. Francis, on the other hand, rather pushed himself forward.'

'And your thoughts on this?' Shute prompted.

'Well, sir. I don't think he pushed her downstairs – if he had, I imagine he'd have stayed tucked away in his room. Plus, he's level-headed. Supposing Rose had screamed as she fell, people would have rushed to see what was happening and there he'd be, the obvious culprit. But if he had reason to think Alice Littleton had caused her to fall, and if he feared Rose might recover and name her assailant, that gives him motive.'

'Quite a few "ifs" there,' Shute observed.

'I know, but we have to start somewhere.'

'True.'

'I thought we'd bring both him and Alice to the station for a formal interview tomorrow.'

'Fine. I'll leave it to you.'

Once Shute had returned to his office, Matt said, 'When we go to Blue Moon in the morning, I think we should speak with Neil and his wife about the "missing" items, see if they can't throw any light on them.'

CHAPTER TWELVE

Paula entered the kitchen in her dressing gown and blearily crossed the room to fill the kettle and prep the coffee maker. She was seriously considering asking Dr Hugh to prescribe some sleeping tablets. She had not had a good night's sleep for a week. Ever since Rose's death, in fact. She stared moodily out of the window until the kettle snapped off. Collecting her small red teapot, she warmed it before scooping in tea leaves and then filling it with boiling water. Leaving it to steep, she turned to lay out the breakfast things.

That was when she saw the folded white paper. With trepidation, fully justified as it turned out, she picked it up and read its contents. Just when she thought life could only improve, it proved her wrong.

When Neil, fully dressed for work, came in she set a freshly brewed mug of coffee in front of him and started the toaster.

'Are you having cereal this morning?' she asked.

'I don't think so. Just toast. I've got quite a bit to do today and I want to make an early start.'

Paula waited until he had a mouthful of toast before delivering yet more bad news. 'When I got down here this morning there was a note from Selina.'

'A note?'

'Yes. Now, I want you to keep calm but she's gone to the music festival with Zoggo.'

'What?'

'Neil, it's a fait accompli. There's nothing we can do about it. And she is over eighteen.'

'Then I wish she'd start to act like it. The least she could have done was talk to us face to face. Ask permission.'

'If she had, would you have granted it?'

'Obviously not. I thought I'd made my feelings about it clear to her.'

'There you are then. She wanted to avoid further conflict.'

'I'll give her conflict when she returns,' he muttered.

'Neil, must I remind you again that she is of age and must be allowed to live her own life. We can advise her but ultimately it's her decision.'

'So we should just stand back and let her waste her life? It's all that Zoggo's fault. He's thrown his life away and is encouraging her to do the same.'

Paula placed her hand over his fist on the table. 'She's intelligent—'

Neil snorted. 'She certainly doesn't flaunt it!'

'As I say, she's intelligent. If she didn't have to constantly defend Zoggo to us, I'm pretty sure she'd move on from him.'

He stared searchingly at her while he weighed up her words. Finally he muttered, 'Okay, I'll try to be more laidback with her.'

She removed her hand to take a much-needed swig of

tea. That had gone better than she had hoped. 'Good,' she managed, and decided to have a slice of toast to celebrate. Small victories could be as gratifying as epic ones.

On reaching his office, Neil extracted the file of people who were on the waiting list to reside at Blue Moon. He did not want another mistake like Rose so spent some time studying their details and the notes of impressions that had been formed at their preliminary visit. Finally, he was ready to contact who he considered would fit in best with the other guests.

Over an hour later he sat back lost in thought. This was how Sonja and Paula found him when they arrived for a coffee break.

'Hello, Neil. Hard at it, I see,' Sonja joked as she went to fill mugs from the percolator.

However, Paula realised as soon as she saw him that something was very wrong. 'Neil? What's happened?' She was afraid some new disaster had befallen them. When on earth would their lives take an upward swing?

Coming out of his contemplative stupor, Neil shrugged as he pushed papers back into the file on his desk. 'Not totally unexpected, I suppose, but still a bit of a shock.'

'Not Selina?' Paula's mouth dried with sudden fear.

'Selina? No, no. Anyway, I'm taking a laissez-faire attitude regarding her now. Isn't that what we decided?'

Ignoring this sally, Paula reiterated, 'What's happened? What's wrong?'

He slapped his hand on the file in front of him. 'No one wants to come here now. Oh, as soon as our killer is caught and removed, then they would be delighted to come. But not before then.' He rose and returned the file to its cabinet. Paula relaxed slightly as she sank into a chair.

'I suppose it's understandable. They don't want to find the person in the room next door might be a dangerous killer.' Sonja brought over the mugs of coffee.

'God,' Neil surged to his feet in frustration, 'it's not as if we have a serial killer or homicidal maniac running loose.'

'No,' Paula agreed quietly. 'But, from their point of view, they can't be sure. I mean, we know that Rose was a blight on our small community here. She clearly pushed someone over the edge. Not that I'm saying that killing her was the best answer, but whoever did, it was probably on the spur of the moment.'

Neil stared at his wife for a long moment before sinking back into his chair and reaching for his coffee. 'When you're right, you're right.' He gave her a small smile. 'That's twice in one day – and it's not even lunch yet!'

Sonja ventured, 'And it's likely the police will sort it all out soon and we'll all be able to get back to normal.'

'Yes,' Paula said. 'Blue Moon is financially stable enough to run with one fewer guest than its full complement. Isn't it?'

'Yes, of course.' Neil looked much more normal now. 'I just wasn't expecting it. But, as you say, it's not for long.' He drank some coffee.

Sonja mused, 'I just hope none of our remaining guests decide to leave.'

'Sonja,' Paula snapped. 'Not helping.'

Sonja appeared surprised at the outburst before realising she could have set Neil back again. 'Of course it won't happen. Our guests are too comfortable, not to mention loyal to Blue Moon, to even consider it.' She swilled back the rest of her coffee. 'Well, I'd better get on, Maria wants to go over the menus for next week.' She rinsed her mug and left the room.

Neil smiled at his wife. 'Don't worry. I've calmed down. Approaching a Zen state any minute.'

She sighed. 'This is turning into a really bloody day.'

'Well, at least it can't get any worse.'

'Don't say that! That's what I thought about Selina's note.'

'Retracted then.' He glanced at a reminder on his desk. 'Inspector Devlin is due here soon. He rang to say he wanted a word with us both.'

'Perhaps he'll have some news for us.'

'Perhaps.' Neil's tone did not sound too confident.

✂⚬✂

As he and Rick drove to Blue Moon, Matt ruminated on his conversation with Esme during the previous evening, when they had just finished eating.

'Esme, there seem to be some items missing from Rose's room like letters, a journal of some sort and money. Do you know anything about them?'

Her face turned stony. 'What are you accusing me of?'

'Oh, for God's sake. I'm not accusing you of anything – and you know it. I just wondered if someone had taken them, maybe for safekeeping, and they'd mentioned it to you.'

'No. And may I remind you we agreed not to talk about Blue Moon or your case.'

'I know, but this is different. I'll also be asking the same thing to various people at Blue Moon in the morning.'

'I hope you don't give the impression you think they were stolen. I know nothing about them and I can't imagine anyone there stealing them.'

'Don't be so frosty. It's a legitimate question under the circumstances.'

'How do you know they're missing? Perhaps they never existed in the first place.'

'Possibly. But most people keep a diary or calendar just as an aide memoir for future events. As for money, people usually have some on hand, but there was none at all, not a penny, nor any credit cards. And what about letters? We know she'd received some, but they're gone too.'

Esme looked pensive. 'She kept letters in a sort of stylised rack. It looked like flowers in a vase at the front. It was on her dressing table. I remember it quite clearly.'

'Okay. That's helpful. Thanks.'

'What do you think happened to them? I can't see they'd be of much, if any, value to anyone else.'

'They're loose ends. It's quite likely there's a perfectly good explanation for why they were removed. But until that's ascertained they're the sort of details that niggle.'

Esme had looked at him for a long moment, then sighed. 'No more about the case.'

'Agreed.' They had started the clearing up and the conversation had moved on to innocuous topics.

On their arrival at Blue Moon the two detectives went straight to the office where Neil and Paula were waiting, as Matt had requested. After the initial pleasantries were out of the way, Matt got straight to the point.

'Do either of you know if, after Rose's death, any items were removed from her room for safekeeping?' There, he thought, Esme should be satisfied that his enquiry contained no hint of nefarious doings!

'Just her handbag,' Paula answered. 'I brought it here. There wasn't much in it. Some pens, tissues and a purse with a little money in it. Mr Bucknell, her nephew, took the money but didn't want the bag, so I added it to the items we took to the charity shop.'

'I see. What about a diary or notebook, or any mail she'd received?'

'I can't recall them.'

'Not to worry.' He smiled at her before turning to her husband. 'Do you know if Peter Francis and Alice Littleton are around?'

Paula stood. 'I'll go and see if I can find them.'

'Thank you.'

Once she had left on her quest, Neil asked, 'Are they in trouble?'

'Probably not.' Matt's reply was insouciant. 'We would like them to accompany us to the station so we can clarify one or two things.'

Neil looked as if he would like to know more, but after a pause contented himself with, 'I see.'

Matt was well aware he did not see but with a single nod acknowledged his restraint.

Neil smiled. 'Naturally I'd like to know more, but under the circumstances I'd rather be able to claim total ignorance to any enquiries!'

Matt smiled appreciatively just as the door opened and Sonja appeared. Seeing Matt, she paused. 'I'm sorry. I'll come back later.'

'Just a second, please.' Neil stopped her. 'Do you recall if Rose had a diary or journal or what she did with the letters she received?'

'She had a book she wrote in. I don't think it was a diary. More like a sort of jotter, if you know what I mean?'

'And her letters?'

'She kept them in a letter holder on her dressing table.'

'Have you any idea what became of them?' Matt asked.

She shook her head. 'No, sorry. I suppose her nephew may have taken them.'

'Thank you. That's very helpful.' Matt sent her a smile which she reciprocated. 'One other thing,' he said, looking at each of them, 'do either of you have any idea why Rose would have been up and about that late?'

Both shook their heads. Sonja added, 'The guests all have a kettle in their rooms if they wish to make a hot drink. No need to go down to the kitchen.'

'I see.' Matt jotted a few words in his notebook.

After a glance at Neil, Sonja retreated from the office, passing Paula, who was on her way in.

'They have been out, but I caught them just as they returned. They'll be here in a minute.'

'That's good.' Matt rose and addressed Neil. 'I'll get out of your way. We'll wait for them outside.'

Paula stared after them. 'I thought they had some questions for Alice and Peter.'

Neil shrugged. 'They do but want to ask them at the police station.'

'Neil! Do they think they, or one of them, killed Rose?'

'I've no idea. Devlin just said it was to clear up a few points.'

'In that case, why can't they ask them here?'

'Paula, love, I've no idea and they weren't being at all forthcoming.'

She sank onto a chair. 'I can't believe it was either of them.'

'It probably wasn't. Devlin didn't say they were under arrest. Just needed to answer some more questions.'

She thought about this. 'I suppose – but you do hear of people "helping police with their enquiries". And then they're free to leave.'

Neil decided to overlook her doubtful tone. 'So there's nothing to worry about.'

Alice and Peter were taken to the police station together. Once there, however, they were separated so dextrously they hardly noticed until they found themselves in separate interview rooms. Matt decided to question Alice first before her nerves stretched so tightly she would be unable to answer coherently.

He smiled reassuringly at her while Rick set the recording mechanism in motion. 'I want you to be clear. You agreed to come here for interview?'

She nodded, her eyes wide with trepidation.

'You know you can leave at any time and, if you wish, you may have a solicitor present?'

'Am I being accused of killing Rose?' Her voice was barely above a whisper.

'No. We only want to ask some questions.'

'I see.'

'It's just that sometimes people recall events more clearly here, than when in familiar surroundings.'

'Oh.'

'Can you tell us again how you felt when Rose was critical of the way the Residents' Association's meetings were conducted?'

'I was upset.'

'Yes?'

'I've already told you, I decided to resign, but Neil and Esme dissuaded me.'

'Do you feel you were dissuaded against your will?'

'Not really. They pointed out, you see, that if I did then Rose may have put herself forward as chair. Well, you can see that would have been disastrous.'

Matt nodded gravely.

'The main thing was when Rose said my being chair was undemocratic as I'd never been elected by the others. But

I was encouraged by the others at the end of the meeting and Wally even said I'd done well.' Her pinkened cheeks revealed how much that had meant to her.

'On the Wednesday of last week, did you get up at all once you'd gone to bed?'

'No.'

'You're quite sure?'

'Of course I am.'

'You see, we wondered if you'd come across Rose on the landing. Perhaps she had another dig at you. You both argued, maybe she was threatening, you pushed her away in self-defence and she lost her balance and fell down the stairs.'

'No!' Alice looked horrified. 'Nothing like that. I never got out of bed. I slept through everything. I knew nothing about it until the next morning.' It was apparent she was working herself into an extremely agitated state.

'All right, Mrs Littleton – Alice. We'll leave that line of questioning.'

'Good,' she said faintly.

Rick intervened. 'Can I get you something? Some water or coffee?'

'No, thank you.' She straightened her shoulders.

Matt tried to look as innocuous as he could. 'Do you have any ideas as to why Rose may have been up and about at that time of night?'

'No idea. How should I know? We weren't friends, as you know. In fact, I don't think she was friends with anyone at Blue Moon.'

'Can you think of anyone who specially didn't like her?'

She met his eyes. 'Yes, everyone. She was a nasty woman.'

'So it seems. Well, that's all for now, Mrs Littleton. Thank you for your cooperation.' The interview concluded.

With Alice again refusing any refreshments, she was taken to a waiting area while Matt and Rick went to the interview room where Peter sat looking irritated by the delay.

'Where's Alice? Is she all right?'

'She's perfectly fine. She elected to wait for you, so we've put her in the waiting area.' Matt sat down and waited for Rick to set up the recording apparatus and go through Peter's rights.

'Now,' Matt started, 'would you tell us how you felt when Rose upset Alice?'

'I've already told you.'

'Please can you tell us again? Sometimes a bit of new information comes forward in a repeated account.'

'I was angry. Who was she to waltz in and cause disruption like that? Anyway, as you know, I offered to write up some meeting notes as a sop to Rose.'

'Did it work?'

'No. She then started on constitutions and that officers should be elected. All that rubbish.'

'That must have made you even more angry.'

'In a way, not so much. It was rather ridiculous for the set-up we have. Also, the others stood up for Alice and our procedures – or rather, lack of them.'

'Mmm. Moving on to the night of Rose's death, why did you go downstairs?'

Peter sighed long-sufferingly. 'Mainly curiosity. I went to see what was happening, met Lucy, who told me that Rose was dead after falling downstairs. I went to see for myself, I suppose.'

'A bit ghoulish, wasn't it?'

Peter shrugged.

'Still, when you got downstairs you found she wasn't dead. At least, not then.'

'No. Celia said Sonja had examined Rose and found she was alive, although a bit damaged. Some broken bones clearly and, of course, she was unconscious.'

'I understand that Miss Foster accompanied Miss Strong upstairs then.'

'That's right.'

'And Mrs Davies was in the office calling the doctor.'

'Yes.'

'So you were alone with Rose?'

'For a short time, yes. Celia returned quite quickly and Sonja also came out of the office.'

'Did you mind being there alone with Rose?'

'Of course not. In fact, I suggested Celia took Lucy upstairs.'

'Really?'

'Yes, really. Lucy gets easily upset. She'd already had a shock when they found Rose. It was better she was got away from the scene.'

'And while you were alone with Rose, what were your thoughts?'

'My thoughts? God, I don't know.'

'Try to remember.'

'Well, I suppose I wondered what had happened. Perhaps that if it had to happen to anyone, she would be my first choice. Sort of just deserts, you know.'

'Perhaps you thought it a pity that she wasn't dead? Following that, maybe you decided to remedy that situation?'

'I didn't kill her.'

'Would you be willing to supply a DNA sample for analysis comparison?'

'I repeat, I did not kill her. But if that's the route you're taking, then I want a solicitor.'

That evening Esme cleared her throat delicately. 'I know we're not going to talk about the case.'

'That's right.'

'I just wondered if you'd managed to rule anyone out yet. I just want to know the people you've set to one side. Note that I didn't ask who you suspected.'

Matt eyed her askance. 'We've just established that we're not talking about the case!'

'Phooey. You asked me about things of Rose's you thought were missing. I helped.'

'Actually, you did. Okay, I can be fair. We're not looking, at the moment, at Neil, Paula, Larry, the cook, Jan, Marj and, possibly, Charles Green.'

She cocked her head in question.

Matt put down the tea towel. 'Neil and Paula lacked opportunity. Plus they wouldn't have wanted this sort of scandal connected to their business. Larry, no opportunity and no motive. The cook, Marj and Jan also had no opportunity – and all three live out. Satisfied?'

'You also said Charles.'

'From all accounts he seems almost disassociated from all the residents. Possibly he was even unaware of Rose's troublemaking.'

She snorted. 'Don't you believe it. He spends a lot of time observing what's going on. I doubt much gets past him.'

'What would be his motive?'

'Oh, a hard one. Let me think. Maybe altruism. For the benefit of the others.'

Matt considered her words, then groaned. 'He'll have to go back to our Possibles list then. Not for the killing, as he didn't have the opportunity, but for the altercation on the stairs. Although, I can't help feeling altruism is rather a weak motive.' He eyed her. 'This isn't helping, you know.'

'Oh, I don't know. Just making sure you're keeping an open mind!'

'Of course there's also the fact that if he really is so observant, it's worth talking to him again about those observations.'

They worked in silence for a couple of minutes.

'Still, Esme, I'm trusting you not to repeat any of this to your pals at Blue Moon.'

'I know, and you can. Trust me, that is.'

CHAPTER THIRTEEN

Outside it was deluging as Paula filled and turned on the kettle for her wake-up cup of tea. She stared out of the window at the dirty grey sheets of rain. It suited her mood. She turned and dropped two slices of bread into the toaster while she wondered how Selina was faring in the middle of a field during this tempest. Still, she comforted herself, it would not be difficult for her to come home if it got too bad.

Settled with her tea, toast and marmalade at the kitchen table, Paula stared into space as she mulled over her overwhelming worry. Neil. One thing after another was hitting Blue Moon and his new "laidback" attitude seemed to be morphing into a frightening "withdrawal".

Waking up around two this morning and finding herself alone, she had gone in search of him. She had found him in the sitting room staring at the wall while music played. He was so lost in his head that he did not hear her say his name and when she had crossed over and put a hand on his shoulder, he had started as if it had been a cattle prod.

'What are you doing down here? Couldn't you sleep?'

'No.'

'Do you want me to make you something?'

'No. Don't fuss, Paula.' He looked up at her. 'Go back to bed. I'm fine. I'll be up soon.'

With no real alternative if she did not want to upset him any further, she had returned to bed, where she had lain awake for over an hour waiting for him. Finally, exhaustion had tipped her into an uneasy sleep.

When she had woken this morning, he was gone. Whether he had come to bed at some time she had no idea but thought it unlikely.

She bit into her toast. Perhaps she would have a word with Hugh. Ask for his professional advice. Of course, the police needed to find their culprits, a new guest installed in Rose's old room and Blue Moon restored to its pre-Rose glory. If not done quickly she would have to take matters into her own hands. She was not going to sit back and let Neil sink totally into the Slough of Despond.

❧❦

Selina sat morosely on her damp sleeping bag in her crumpled clothes. This was not at all how she had envisaged her first music festival to play out.

They had arrived the previous afternoon, found a spot for their tents but only then discovered none of them knew how to erect them. This had resulted in a fair bit of cursing, blame-laying as well as a little blood. The drummer of Zoggo's group, Mark, had managed to pinch a couple of fingers, breaking the skin. Selina sniffed. Honestly, the carry on, you would have thought he had completely severed the fingers. Then going on about getting his hands insured at the first opportunity – so long as he was still able to play, that is. It had not helped to find out that many of the festival-goers came without any tents and bought a cheap version that appeared to just need throwing onto the ground to make them self-erect. In the end, two chaps who had been watching their antics came over and the tents were up in no time at all. Otherwise, no doubt, they would still not be up and they would have slept under the sky – and rain.

Later Frank had been dispatched to forage some supper for everyone. By the time he returned, both the burgers and chips were cool and soggy. Irritatingly, he had already eaten his food while chatting with some friends he bumped into. No doubt they had then still been hot and edible.

However, the rest of the evening had been good as they had joined the crowds listening to one performer after another. But, once they had retired, she had lain uncomfortable in her damp sleeping bag staring into the darkness, unable to sleep. Hunger pangs had not helped either. Still, at some point she must have dropped off because when she woke it was to find herself deserted. Not one of the band members had even bothered to leave a note.

Wallowing in self-righteous misery, she whipped her head round as the opener of the tent zipped down. Zoggo's face appeared, but before he could utter a word she snapped, 'Where the hell have you been?'

Scrambling in, Zoggo looked surprised at her greeting. 'Round and about. We've met some really interesting people.'

'Good for you. Did you not think I might have liked to come with you?'

'Not really. You were asleep. Thought it best to let you get a good rest.'

'A good rest? Zoggo, they're about to start playing!'

'That's why I came back. Some of the stages are about ready to start. Thought you wouldn't want to miss them.'

Selina looked at his face, her ire deflating. He really had considered he had been thoughtful. 'Okay. But don't go off again leaving me alone.'

'Got ya. Come on then, we don't want to miss anything.'

She clambered out after him. 'We'll need to get some breakfast. Last night's meal, well, least said. I'm starving.'

'Oh, okay. Well, we'll be by stage two when you've finished.'

'Don't you want something to eat?'

'Nope. The boys and I had a full fry-up from one of the concessions when we first got up and we've just had fish and chips. I'm stuffed.'

She gaped in disbelief. 'Why didn't you fetch me before getting these fish and chips?'

'Meant to, but the food van was on the way. And the boys and I were hungry, so…'

She shook her head. 'At least you can now keep me company while I get some food.'

He frowned. 'Why?'

'As I said, to keep me company.'

'But the first set is about to start.'

'Fine, if that's more important to you than coming with me.'

He grinned. 'That's my girl. See you later then.' He bussed her cheek and bounded off to, presumably, stage two. She watched as he disappeared amongst the horde of wandering music aficionados.

'Unbelievable,' she muttered before slogging off in search of much-needed sustenance.

৶৽৾

On her arrival at Blue Moon, Esme was waylaid by Peter even before she had fully passed through the front door. Clearly he had been lying in wait for her.

'Esme, please can you see Alice? I'm so worried about her.'

'Alice? She's not ill, is she?'

'No. Maybe. Probably not. Not really.'

Well, that was clear, she thought as she put a hand on his arm. 'Peter, let's find some privacy and sit down. Then you can explain the problem.'

He allowed himself to be led into the dining room, empty at this time of day. They sat down.

'Now, what's the problem?'

He took a deep breath. 'You probably know that Alice and I were taken to the police station yesterday…'

'What?'

'Yes, to be questioned. Anyway, as soon as we arrived they separated us. I was left twiddling my thumbs while they grilled Alice.'

'This was Matt and Rick?'

'I can understand your surprise. When they questioned people here, they were so polite and considerate. But at the station, everything was different. I don't know what they said to Alice, but when my turn came they accused me of killing Rose and said they wanted a DNA sample from me.'

'And when you saw Alice next she was upset?'

'Upset? One way to put it, I suppose. As soon as we got back here she went straight to her room and spent the rest of the day in bed. Refused to eat anything or talk about her interview with the police.'

'What about this morning? Did she come down for breakfast?'

'No. She's still in her room. Esme, she hasn't eaten anything since breakfast yesterday. I've tried talking with her. So have Sonja and Paula, but all to no avail.'

'Okay, I'll try my luck. I'll just deposit my bag in the office, then go straight up.'

'Thank you. You're my last hope. Sonja's talking about calling for Dr Saunders but she agreed to hold off until I'd spoken to you.'

Esme paused. 'Peter, I can't promise anything, you know.'

He nodded. 'I'm just hoping she'll talk to you, partly because she really likes you and partly because of your relationship with Devlin.'

'I see.' She opened the door then looked back. 'Did you give them a sample of your DNA?'

'Certainly not. Told them I wanted a solicitor. That brought the interview to an end.'

Esme smiled as she headed to the office. A few minutes later she tapped on Alice's door. 'Alice? It's me, Esme. May I come in?'

There was a long pause before she heard a begrudging, 'It's not locked.'

Taking that as an invitation, Esme went in. Alice was lying on her side, facing away from the door. Esme walked round the bed and drew up a chair.

'Peter tells me you and he went to the police station yesterday.'

No response of any kind.

'Obviously it greatly upset you. Can you tell me about it?'

The silence stretched until Esme started to think she would have no more luck than the rest of them. Then Alice spoke, so quietly that Esme had to lean forward to hear. 'Your Matt thinks I pushed Rose down the stairs.'

'Oh, Alice…'

'You weren't there. But that's what he said. Esme, I didn't like Rose, I don't think anyone did.'

'That's true.'

'The thing is,' Alice pulled herself to a sitting position. 'When your Matt questioned me before, I told him I'd wished she'd go. I didn't mean,' she hastened to explain, 'that I wanted her dead. Just gone from here.'

'I understand.'

'Well, obviously your Matt thinks it meant I tried to kill her.' She looked miserable.

'No, I don't think so.'

'Esme, he said it.'

'Did he say he thought you'd pushed Rose, or did he ask you if you did?'

'What's the difference?'

'The first means he thinks you did, or if he asked it could be he was just trying to see your reaction.'

'I can't think now if he asked.'

'Did he realise how upset you were?'

'I don't know. Probably not, I answered other questions after.'

'I'm pretty sure he doesn't think you pushed Rose. If he did, I think he'd have kept you at the station under the suspicion you had.'

Alice visibly brightened as she considered this. 'I think you're right. I can't believe why I didn't think of that.'

Esme patted her hand. 'You were too involved.'

'Yes.' She mulled it over. 'I think it was when I was on my own while they questioned Peter. There was nothing to do but wait and I kept going over and over it. I was so frightened I was going to end up in prison. I mean, how would I have been able to face my children – or anyone here?'

She was starting to become distressed again so Esme

clasped her hand. 'That's not happening, so don't even think about it anymore.'

'You're right. I'm so stupid. I suppose everyone here is talking about me.'

'They're worried about you. They like you, you're their friend. Especially Peter.'

Alice flushed. 'Yes, he's a very good friend.'

'So, no more brooding?'

'No.'

'Shall I ask Peter to come and see you now?'

'No.' Alice was firm. 'I'll get dressed and come down.'

'That's the spirit. I'll leave you to it then. I'd better go and do some work! I know he'll be waiting to hear how you are. I'll tell him you'll be down shortly, shall I?'

'Yes.'

Matt and Rick reported to Frank Shute first thing that morning. The problem was they did not have anything concrete to put forward.

Shute encapsulated the situation. 'What we have is all circumstantial. No proof nor hard evidence centred on one person.'

Matt nodded. 'It's still wide open on who pushed the victim. But at least the killer must be either Celia, Peter or Sonja. Sonja is the least likely as she ascertained Rose was not dead from the fall.'

'Outside possibilities are Dr Saunders and Neil Carstairs. However, they were never alone with Rose and neither had motive.'

Shute absorbed this. 'So you'll be concentrating on Celia Foster and Peter Francis?'

'Mmm.' Matt was lost in thought. The other two, recognising this, waited patiently. 'I know we removed Charles Green from our list of possible suspects, but something Esme told me last night keeps preying on my mind.'

'Yes?' Shute encouraged.

'She said Green was an observer. Where we saw him as a loner, disassociated from everybody else there, in fact, he probably knew more about what was going on than anyone else.'

'So?' Rick asked.

'So, I think it's worth interviewing him again. Not as a suspect so much as a mine of information on the others.'

'Worth a shot,' Shute agreed.

'If we can get him to talk,' Rick muttered. 'He wasn't exactly a chatty charley before.'

'Oh, very witty,' Matt said as they left Shute's office. 'We can but try.'

Once in the office at Blue Moon, with Charles retrieved, the informal interview commenced. For about half an hour Charles answered their questions amenably while managing not to give the detectives any new information.

Finally, Matt decided to abandon finesse. 'In your opinion, who do you think was responsible for Rose's fall?'

'It would just be guesswork on my side.'

'I realise that, and it's not as if we will immediately arrest whoever you say.'

'Well…' Charles seemed to be thinking hard.

After a long pause, Rick prompted, 'You must have wondered about someone, or even two someones, as being possibles.'

'That's it, really. It's only my speculations. I wouldn't feel right setting you on someone who most likely will turn out to have had nothing to do with it.'

'All right.' Matt let him off that hook before asking, 'Who do think smothered Rose?'

'Ah well. The field is quite narrow for that.'

'Yes, only a few people were alone with Rose and therefore had the opportunity.'

'Exactly.'

'So,' Rick pushed, 'who is your front runner?'

'From what I've gathered, it's most likely either Peter or Celia.'

Matt sighed. 'Out of the two of them, who would you pick?'

'Both could have a motive, similar ones. But I couldn't speculate. It wouldn't be right. Specially if it turned out to be neither of them! It's best I leave you, with your experience, to sort it all out.'

Realising they were not going to squeeze anything helpful from Charles, Matt thanked him for his time and sent him on his way. Alone with his partner, he mused, 'Odd man.'

'He certainly didn't tell us anything, that's for sure.' Rick was disgruntled.

'Not obviously, anyway.'

'What do you mean?'

Matt looked at his partner. 'He was noticeably more relaxed when making conjectures, or not making them, as it turned out, on Rose's killer. He was much more guarded over who may have pushed her. Makes me think he either knows, or strongly suspects, who it was.'

Rick blew out a breath. 'He's protecting someone.'

'Yup. The big question is who.' Silence prevailed, with both men lost in their thoughts until Matt broke it. 'I know we decided to concentrate on Francis and Celia Foster, but I think I'd like to go over a few things with some of the others, if they're around.'

'Who in particular?'

Matt flipped a couple of pages in his notebook. 'Jane Masters, Penny Child, and the Messrs Pargeter, Dunns, Abbott and West.'

'I'll go and see if I can rattle any of them up. It's pretty ropey weather so I shouldn't think they've gone for a walk.'

They were in luck as all six were on the premises and willing to be further interviewed. In fact, Rick had the impression it would provide a welcome diversion for some of them. Well, he thought philosophically, whatever works.

They decided to see West and Abbott together on the basis it was unlikely either had anything further to contribute and neither was a viable suspect. Their prediction panned out with the detectives having learned nothing when Wally and Al left the office, despite neither of them being their usual taciturn selves. Matt summed it up. 'Difficult to know who was interviewing whom!'

Rick grinned in agreement before searching out the next interviewee. Penny was their choice.

'Can Jane and I go in together?' she asked.

Rick hesitated.

Jane shot him a hard stare. 'You saw Wally and Al together. Why should we be any different?'

Giving in gracefully, he ushered the two women into the office. If Matt was surprised to see both of them, he hid it well.

The interview proceeded on expected grounds until Matt asked, 'Both of you slept through without hearing anything?'

'Yes, that's right.' Jane's voice was matter-of-fact.

No response came from Penny, so Matt raised an eyebrow in her direction. She looked unsure but responded, 'I did get up once. I was thirsty and got a glass of water.'

'From where?'

'From the sink in my room.'

'What time was this?'

'I've no idea but I remember I did hear voices.'

'Whose voices?'

'I'm pretty sure one was Rose but I couldn't make out the other.'

'Was it a man or woman?'

'Oh, a man, definitely.'

'What did they say?'

She made a moue. 'I couldn't hear words, just the buzz of talking. To be honest, I wasn't that interested and took my water back to bed.'

'Why didn't you mention this when we interviewed you previously?'

'I'd completely forgotten about it until you asked just now.'

Matt eyed her sceptically. 'When you heard about Rose the following day, you didn't remember hearing her the night before?'

'No,' she said simply.

In the small silence that followed, Jane cleared her throat. 'It was a shock, Inspector, hearing the news. None of us liked her particularly, but we didn't wish her dead.'

The interview wound up shortly afterwards and Larry and Bob, maintaining the two-at-a-time theme, replaced the women. Unfortunately they had nothing new to add, not to the surprise of either Matt or Rick.

Matt went in search of Esme to touch base before leaving but ran into Paula instead.

'Thank you,' he said. 'For allowing us to usurp you from your office once again.'

'Oh, that's no problem. The only one who would have

been using it is your Esme and she's been taken up with Alice.'

At his enquiring expression, she explained, 'Alice was rather traumatised after her visit to your station yesterday and hasn't left her room since.'

'I see.' Matt had a sinking feeling he was going to hear about this when he got home tonight. 'Well, we're off now. Leave you in peace and, again, thank you for your cooperation.'

CHAPTER FOURTEEN

Selina had taken her time over breakfast. She had met a couple of girls and they chatted together while they ate. The food and the relaxing conversation mollified her anger with Zoggo and she set off to find him.

However, when she finally caught up with him it was to find the four band members well down the path to drunkenness. Zoggo spied her and smiled broadly.

'Hey, babe.' He flung an arm over her shoulders and pulled her into his side. She turned her head away from the pungent alcoholic fumes accompanying his words.

'You're drunk.'

'Not quite yet. Still working on it.' He laughed.

'Don't you think it's a bit early?'

'Don't be so prudish. Anyway, look around you, I'm not the only one. After all, we're here to have fun.'

Although she found it hard to believe possible, the afternoon only deteriorated further. As the boys drank more, they found their inane jokes wildly funny, while she began to wonder why she was there. Not even the music, and some of it was seriously good, was enough to counter-balance the boys' antics.

The final straw came back at their tents in the late afternoon. They had gone there so Frank could change his T-shirt after he threw up over the one he was wearing.

'Next stop we'll go to stage four. The Jumping Beans will be on soon,' said Mark.

Selina raised her head. 'I thought we were going to see the Red Lobsters.'

'Not me,' said Mark. 'What about you, Z?'

Zoggo shook his head. 'Mark wants to see the Jumping Beans 'cos their drummer is really supposed to be something else,' he explained to Selina.

'Can't he go and see them then, while we listen to the Red Lobsters?'

'The thing is, babe, I'd rather see the Beans.'

Without a word Selina crawled into the tent. To her surprise, Zoggo followed. She turned to face him.

'Do you ever think about me? What I want?'

He looked puzzled. 'Course. I brought you here, didn't I?'

'And what a treat it's turned out to be!'

'Look, it wasn't easy, you know. The others thought you'd be a drag. But I stood up for you. A real bummer, 'cos it turns out you are a bloody drag. Always complaining. I have to say I'm getting mighty sick of it.'

'News flash. So am I.' Selina dragged her rucksack towards her and began to stuff her belongings into it.

'What are you doing?'

'Packing. I've had enough of you and your pals.'

There was a pause before Zoggo replied, 'If that's how you feel, babe. See you around, then.' He left the tent.

Selina slumped onto the ground and sat alone listening to Zoggo murmur something before they all walked off. Tears fell as she wallowed in her self-righteous misery.

Once they had dried up, she finished her packing, ripped off the festival wristband and left.

⋙⋘

Sonja walked up to the front door and rang the bell before her nerves got the better of her. The door opened and she stared up at Hugh's face.

'I shouldn't be here. I don't know why I phoned you. I'm sorry.' She turned to leave.

Hugh's hand on her arm stayed her departure. 'Look, you're clearly upset. You need someone to talk to.'

She nodded. 'But I shouldn't take advantage of you like that.'

He smiled. 'I'm honoured and thrilled you thought of me at such a time.' He winked. 'I see it as a great breakthrough!'

She chuckled in spite of herself and felt the tension easing its grip on her emotions. She relaxed slightly. Before she knew what was happening she found herself divested of her coat and led into a spacious sitting room. She looked around in curiosity as she settled onto the sofa.

'Your house is lovely.'

'You sound surprised.'

'Not surprised. It's just as I imagined and yet not at all. If you know what I mean?'

'Not really.' He handed her a glass before sitting next to her with his own drink. 'But now's not the time to discuss my home. What's upset you?'

After a last hesitation, she capitulated, 'It's a number of things – I don't know, it all suddenly got too much for me and I had to get away for a bit.'

Hugh nodded and gestured for her to continue.

She gave a nervous laugh. 'I'm not sure where to begin.'

'Anywhere.'

'Okay.' She thought a moment. 'Alice and Peter were taken to the police station yesterday. I don't know exactly what transpired but when Alice got back she retreated to her bed. Wouldn't talk to anyone and refused to eat.'

'Do you want me to see her?'

'No.' She patted his hand unconsciously. 'That at least seems to be resolving itself. She opened up to Esme this morning and is now getting back to normal.'

'That's good.'

'Yes. Then there's Paula. She's worrying herself sick about Neil. This whole Rose debacle is seriously affecting the business, which in turn is affecting his stress levels which is what's worrying her.'

'I see.'

'That's why I felt I couldn't talk to her, even though she's my best friend. Not to mention, from a selfish point of view, if the business does collapse, I lose not just my job but my home as well. And with no income, how will I pay Fred's university tuition?'

It looked as if Hugh was about to speak, but she went on quickly. 'The atmosphere there is worse than when Rose was around.'

'That's certainly saying something!'

'I know. But then at least the guests had a common scapegoat. Now they're all looking at each other, wondering which one of them is the killer.'

There was a long pause before Hugh shifted. 'It's bad now, but the police will sort it out eventually and then life at Blue Moon will be able to settle back into normality. Probably take some time, but things will improve.'

'I just wish they'd get on with it,' was her fierce response.

Hugh put an arm around her and pulled her against

him. They stayed like that for a while until Hugh realised she was weeping.

He tightened his arm. 'Come on, darling. Even if in the unlikely event everything implodes, you won't be alone. I'm always here for you. You know that, don't you?'

She nodded.

'Sonja. You do know that?'

'Yes,' she hiccupped.

'There's something else worrying you. What is it?'

Just when he thought she was not going to answer, he heard a soft whisper.

'What was that?' He pulled back to look into her woebegone face.

'I think the police suspect me.'

'Suspect you?' He frowned.

'Of killing Rose.'

'That's ridiculous.'

'It's not. I'm one of only three people who was left alone with Rose. Only we three had the opportunity.'

'In that case it's one of the other two.'

She gave a broken laugh. 'Oh, Hugh. Such faith in me!'

'You'd better believe it. We'll get through this together. You must remember you are not alone. You've got me.'

'I do believe, I do,' she said softly as she snuggled against him again. She was so tired and he made her feel so safe.

છ∼જી

When Matt arrived home he was met with no signs of supper cooking and a belligerent Esme waiting for him. Assessing the situation quickly, he shrugged off his jacket.

'Hello, sweetheart.' He made a point of sniffing the air. 'Are we having take-out this evening?'

'How could you, Matt?'

'How could I what?'

'Don't play stupid. We both know you're not. I'm referring to your treatment of Alice Littleton yesterday.'

He looked perplexed. 'My treatment?'

'Yes. You dragged her and Peter to the police station. There you accused her of pushing Rose down the stairs and him of finishing her off.'

Matt sighed as he sank onto a chair. 'Firstly, we did not "drag" them anywhere. We drove them to the station, interviewed them then drove them back to Blue Moon. Neither did we accuse them of anything, just outlined possible scenarios. Normal established procedure.'

She stared at him. He looked back impassively.

'Your normal established procedure resulted in Alice retreating to her bed as soon as she got back and refusing to talk to anyone or eat anything. She was traumatised, Matt. She's a gentle person and felt brow-beaten by you.'

'Oh, for goodness' sake. She was not brow-beaten, nor did we pull her fingernails off to force a confession.'

'She had nothing to confess.'

'That's what we decided, so we didn't arrest her!'

'Matt,' her tone was slightly more conciliatory, 'I don't think you realise how threatened people can feel when being questioned at the station. I know from my own experience how gruelling and frightening it can be.'

'That was quite different. Marshall crossed the line with you. But I thought we'd put all that behind us.'

'Yes, we have.' Esme's shoulders slumped. 'She really was frightened yesterday and withdrew from everyone – even Peter. When I talked with her, it brought back my experience of being grilled.'

He patted his knee and she slowly walked over and sat

on it. 'I'm sorry it brought it all back to you. But honestly, we were not harsh on Alice. In fact, as soon as she appeared a bit agitated we tried to soothe her. When she left she seemed completely okay.'

'Yes, I expect she did. I think it was while she was waiting for Peter that she brooded – imagining going to prison, how her family would take it, that sort of thing.'

'Would you like me to visit tomorrow and reassure her?'

'No.' She laughed. 'The best thing would be to keep a healthy distance from her.'

They remained in a comfortable silence that was eventually broken by Esme. 'How is Detective Sergeant Marshall anyway? Is she coming to grips with George's death?' Fiona Marshall's lover, George, had been one of those killed in the Holtexim case.

Matt shrugged. 'Work helps, I think.' After a pause he added, 'So, are we having take-out tonight? I'm starving.'

CHAPTER FIFTEEN

On Saturday morning, just as Paula sat down to eat her toast, she heard footsteps approaching. She sighed. She had hoped Neil would sleep for a bit longer. He certainly had not managed much rest over the last few days. The door opened and she looked up. For a moment she was transfixed, then rose abruptly as Selina entered the kitchen. She rushed to enfold her daughter in a heartfelt embrace.

'When did you get back? Why are you back so early? Are you all right?'

'Of course I'm all right.' The words were of a long-suffering teenager, but the reciprocal hug was tight.

Paula pulled back. 'I'll get you a tea. You put some toast on.' In no time they were both settled at the table.

'What's wrong?' Paula asked gently.

Selina pulled a face. 'Let's just say Zoggo showed a different side of himself. A side I'm not keen on.'

'I'm sorry.'

Selina nodded. 'So am I. I'll just have to chalk it up to experience.' She bit into her toast.

Paula observed her closely. She had been hurt but was proving remarkably resilient. She would be all right. 'When did you get in?'

'Not sure exactly, but before eleven.'

'Did you all come back?'

'No. As far as I know, Zoggo and the boys are still there.'

'A bit late for the buses. How did you get back – in a taxi?'

Selina shook her head. 'Not enough money and I didn't feel like walking that far in the dark, so I hitched.'

Paula swallowed hard, trying not to think of how that might have turned out. The kitchen door swung open as Neil entered. He stopped short on catching sight of his daughter.

Selina stared back for a moment then, rising, she ran into her father's arms. 'Oh, Dad.'

He held her firmly as the two embraced. Paula rose quietly and left the kitchen. The two of them needed privacy.

In the Blue Moon dining room there was a muted buzz of conversation as the residents tucked into their breakfasts. Celia and Lucy were at their usual table.

'I was thinking,' said Celia. 'It's been rather claustrophobic lately, what with everyone wondering which of us did for Rose and the police putting a damper on us all.'

'You're right about that.' Lucy sipped her coffee. 'I still don't see why we couldn't get away. We could at least have gone to a local hotel, as the police apparently don't want us to leave the area.'

'I don't think it would have been a good move. But what I was thinking, there's no reason we shouldn't go out for a break.'

'What sort of break?'

'I thought we could go out for dinner. Maybe see a film or something. Just to have a few hours away from here and the terrible atmosphere. You know, to cheer us up a bit.'

Lucy appeared to be considering it, then shook her head. 'No. I don't want to. We'd still have to come back. Supposing someone else was killed and we found them again. No, I'd be worrying about it all the time we were out.'

Celia stared at her. 'What are the chances someone else would be killed?'

'I don't know, but I don't want to take the risk.' On occasion, Lucy could be very stubborn.

'There is no risk.' Her friend was exasperated.

'How do you know?'

'Because the likelihood is non-existent.'

'You can't say that. You don't know who the killer is, let alone what they might do.'

'Look around you. Does anyone look like they're planning a murder?'

'No. But one of them already has and they say it's easier after the first.'

'Who says that?'

'I don't know, it's just a known fact.'

'You're being ridiculous.'

'And I don't see how you can be so sure they won't decide to strike again.'

Having reached an impasse, they were silent. Eventually, Celia refilled her teacup. 'It was just a thought.'

Lucy gave her a long considering look before getting on with her cornflakes. She screwed up her nose, they'd gone soggy now but she never had liked to waste food.

Across the room, Peter and Alice were sharing a table with Al and Wally.

Wally smiled at Alice. 'Good to see you've recovered.'

Alice became a little flustered. To give herself something to do, she picked up the teapot and filled everyone's cup with tea. She said, 'I'm getting a bit worried about our anniversary celebration. We haven't really made any progress on our plans.'

Peter sloshed milk over his cereal. 'It's probably not the right time just now. Everyone is too preoccupied with the demise of Rose.'

Wally frowned. 'Rum business.'

'Umm,' was Al's contribution to the conversation.

'Yes, of course,' Alice said faintly.

Peter patted her hand in comfort as Wally said, 'The police seem to be going round in circles and getting nowhere.'

'Probably eliminated a few of us, though,' Al said.

'I suppose,' Wally agreed. 'I wish they'd share what information they do have a bit more.'

Peter scooped up the last of his cereal. 'At least none of you are prime suspects.'

'Meaning?' Wally asked.

'If you think about it, there's only Celia, Sonja and me that had the opportunity to kill Rose. No one else was alone with her.'

'Oh, Peter.' Alice was visibly distressed. 'No, surely not.'

He smiled. 'Don't worry. I didn't do it.'

'I know that!'

Wally looked straight at Peter. 'Just not being guilty isn't nearly enough. We've all read about miscarriages of justice.'

'Oh, God,' whispered Alice.

Peter cocked his head in Alice's direction. 'I think we should change the subject. Not conducive to good digestion!'

'Quite so,' agreed Al.

However, Wally added, 'You're right. But I'd just like to put forward a suggestion. We could start our own investigation.'

'But we haven't the experience.' Alice just wanted the whole disaster rolled up and put out of sight and mind.

'No,' Wally smiled at her, 'but we have much better knowledge about everyone here and of the dynamics of living here before Rose, during Rose and now. That gives us an advantage.'

'Suppose so,' supported Al.

Peter was looking thoughtful. 'But why would any of them want to answer our questions?'

Wally shrugged. 'We wouldn't interrogate them like the police. Just get into conversations with them. No surprise if the investigation crops up, it seems to be the main activity and topic at the moment.'

'Natural,' agreed Al.

'It's certainly an idea.' Peter was coming round to the concept – probably, not least, as he would be actively working to clear himself. He looked at Alice. 'How about it? Shall we have a go at sleuthing?'

Tentatively she returned his smile. 'All right, if you think it's a good idea.'

'If nothing else, it'll give us something to do. All this waiting around is driving us nuts.'

'Yes,' her voice was stronger. 'And we need to make sure you don't get arrested.'

'That's my girl.'

Alice flushed slightly while Wally and Al exchanged expressive looks.

Al said, 'We'll see what we can glean as well, eh, Wally?'

Wally nodded. 'We can share a table again at supper

and compare our findings.' That settled, the quartet concentrated on finishing their breakfast.

めでる

At the police station Matt and Rick reported to the SIO. The three glumly surveyed the whiteboard covered in facts gleaned so far in the investigation.

'Well?' Shute prodded.

Matt straightened. 'I'm convinced Charles Green knows, or at least strongly suspects, something. But he's not prepared to tell us.'

'Have you removed him completely from your pool of suspects?'

'We have for the murder, he had no opportunity,' Rick said.

'That's right,' Matt agreed. 'He's a loner and a quiet one, but I can't knock him off the list of possibles who pushed Rose. It's the quiet ones that often have the worst tempers. He could have pushed her in the heat of the moment.'

Rick added, 'Penny Childs heard Rose arguing that night and says it was with a man. This would appear to exonerate Alice as well as all the other women.'

Shute queried, 'Were you thinking of Alice as the pusher?'

'We considered Peter as the killer. He had the opportunity but the only motive we could come up with was that he knew, or suspected, Alice had pushed Rose and, presented with the chance, he killed her so she could not place the blame on Alice.'

Matt added, 'Of course, if he suspected Alice had done that, it leaves his motive open. Not to mention, if he was the one arguing with Rose, he was also the only man left alone with her.'

'I suppose it would be a tidy result – one person responsible for both actions.'

'Life is rarely accommodating like that, sir.' Matt grinned.

'No.' Shute mused for a few moments. 'So to sum up, where are you now?'

Matt stared at the board. 'I feel the key underlying all of this is protectiveness. Peter protecting Alice. Celia protective of Lucy. Larry protective of Penny. Jane and Robert – I can think of no motive, both are rather absorbed in their own interests. As for Wally and Al, again no motive. Sonja Davies, we can find no motive other than dislike or maybe frustration but, like Neil and Paula, she would be aware of the possible consequences of scandal on the business.'

'So again not likely,' agreed Shute.

'However,' Matt continued, 'on the positive side, we have whittled down the number of viable suspects. Also, I don't feel we're mindlessly running around in a fog. I can feel a pattern emerging. It's just not clear, as yet.'

'Good.' Shute turned towards his office. 'Maybe you need to step back from it and return refreshed. Clear up any outstanding paperwork this morning then go home.'

'Thank you, sir,' both officers chorused as, grinning, they returned to their desks.

❧

It was late morning when Blue Moon received a visitor in the form of Edward Masters. Neil and Paula were in the office when he arrived. The couple remembered him clearly from when he accompanied his mother to look over Blue Moon. A rather pompous man whose main concern seemed to have been the fees.

They sat him down and offered coffee, which he refused. 'I'll come straight to the point. I'm very concerned for my mother's safety. As far as I can gather from various press reports, one of your guests killed another and as yet the police have been unable to identify the killer. Is that correct?'

Neil nodded. 'Of course, it's only a matter of time before they sort it all out.'

'Maybe so. However, it doesn't alter the fact that in the meantime my mother is living in an establishment where there's a murderer on the loose.'

'I can give you the name and contact details of the investigating officer, if you'd like.'

'Not particularly, no. I think my mother needs to be removed from any danger. That's why I'm here.'

Before Neil could respond, Paula intervened. 'Does your mother know about this?'

'Not exactly, no. I've spoken with her about recent events here but not specifically about her moving out. With me here, though, I'm sure she will agree.'

Paula smiled sweetly. 'Let's call her in, then. After all, this most directly affects her.'

He frowned but nodded. 'Of course.'

'I'll try to track her down then. I'll be as quick as I can.' She left the two men together in an uncomfortable silence.

True to her word, Paula returned shortly with Jane Masters in tow.

'What's this all about, Edward?'

He stood and kissed her cheek. 'Mother.'

'Well?'

'I'm worried about your welfare living here with an unidentified killer roaming freely around. Madeleine and I thought it would be better if you came to stay with us, at least until this whole mess is cleared up.'

'Nonsense. I'm perfectly all right. Why would anyone want to get rid of me?' She paused a beat. 'Apart from your lovely wife, of course.'

Her son flushed. He was only too well aware there was no love lost between his domineering wife and forceful mother. 'Perhaps we could discuss this in private?'

'There's no point. I've no intention of leaving Blue Moon.'

'But the danger—'

'Does Madeleine know about this plan of yours?'

'Of course,' he assured her virtuously. 'And she is of the same mind as me.'

She looked sceptical. Then her face cleared. 'Of course, you're thinking to use this opportunity to get me away from here. Perhaps you were hoping to charge me for room and board at your house?'

By now, scarlet in the face, Edward glanced at Paula and Neil, who were watching the exchange with great interest.

'Mother, we can go into the finer details later. At present I'm just trying to ensure your safety.'

'No need. I'm settled here and have no intention of leaving.'

'But, Mother—'

'Do be sensible, Edward. In no time at all Madeleine and I would be at loggerheads, you'd be miserable – more miserable than any boarding fee would ameliorate. And that's not taking into account my feelings. I'm going to stay here with my friends. Not to mention I'm pretty sure the police would rather we all stay put until their investigation is complete.'

He stared at her, then shrugged. 'If that's the way you feel, there's nothing I can do.'

'No, there isn't.' She walked towards the door with her son following.

'Don't blame me if you're attacked,' he warned.

'I shan't,' she replied cheerfully. 'And, Edward, don't worry, even if I lived several more decades here, there will still be plenty for you to inherit.'

'Mother!'

The door closed shutting off their voices. Paula and Neil looked at each other. After a couple of moments they both exploded into laughter.

☙❧

The phone rang about mid-afternoon; Esme answered it, 'Hello. Oh. Hi, Marcia. How's it going?'

She listened. 'This evening?' She caught Matt's eye. 'You'd like us to come for an early supper?'

Matt nodded at her.

'We'd love to come. What time? Okay. See you then.' Esme disconnected the call.

'Any time after six, she said. Also it's supper – no dressing up.'

'Suits me.' Matt smiled. 'It was a short call. Usually the two of you chat for ages.'

'Yes.' Esme pondered. 'I suppose she thought we could natter this evening.'

'Mmm.'

'Matt, she sounded different. A bit hyper. I hope nothing's wrong.'

'It can't be that bad if she's giving us supper.'

'Not bad, exactly. You don't think Peter's firm is sending him abroad, do you?'

'I've no idea. I've not spoken with him since that evening we got together.'

'I do hope they don't. Naturally, Marcia would go with him. I'd really miss her.' Esme looked despondent.

'For heaven's sake, Esme. We've no idea what, if anything, has happened. Sheesh. Talk about borrowing trouble!'

'I know something's up, something she didn't want to tell me over the phone.'

Matt went up to her and lifted her chin on his hand. 'Don't fret. Say, he has been offered a project overseas, he'd love it. So would Marcia, I expect. Nowadays you're not cut off from people in other parts of the world. You can phone or Skype. And, anyway, it wouldn't be for ever.'

She smiled slightly. 'You're right. And if they went for a long time, perhaps we could visit them.'

'There you go, love. Much better to look for the positives!'

It was nearing half past six when Esme and Matt arrived. As they walked up to the house, they could see Marcia, her short, white-blonde hair sticking out in all directions as if she'd repeatedly run her fingers through it, framed in the open doorway.

'You're right,' Matt said sotto voce to Esme. 'Something is definitely up.'

'And from her face it's hard to tell if it's good or bad news.'

At the door Esme hugged her friend and Matt kissed her cheek.

'Is everything all right?' Esme queried.

Peter loomed up behind his wife. 'Come in, come in. Hope you're both hungry as Marcia's been cooking up a storm.'

'Great.' Matt passed the women and entered the house.

'Marcia,' Peter said. 'Let them come in first.'

'Of course. Of course. Come in, Esme.'

Esme trailed Matt into the sitting room. Very quickly

Peter sorted drinks for everyone before going to stand beside his wife and placing an arm round her shoulders. 'Okay, better let it out before you burst.'

With all eyes suddenly trained on her, it seemed to make Marcia freeze. But only for a moment. 'We've got news and I wanted to tell you in person.' She looked at each of them. Esme thought she would be the one to explode with tension if Marcia did not get on with it.

Marcia gave a tremulous smile. 'We're pregnant.'

'Oh, Marcia. How wonderful.' Esme rushed over to give her a big hug as Matt slapped Peter on the back with congratulations. 'When is it due?'

'Not till the new year.'

'You must be so excited.'

'Ye-es. I am pleased but at the same time quite nervous about it.'

'That's normal,' Esme assured her based on her zero experience of pregnant women.

'Do you really think so?' Marcia began to relax.

The rest of the evening passed in a haze of plans while they demolished the veritable mountain of food Marcia had prepared.

On their way home Esme said, 'It is lovely, isn't it? I think they'll make great parents.'

Matt grunted, 'At least it should keep her out of trouble.'

'What on earth do you mean?'

'I'll just say one word: blackmail.'

'Oh, good grief, Matt. She only did that to help me.'

He gave her a stony stare. Unfortunately for him, it did not generate the response he wanted as Esme broke into giggles.

It was after midnight when Matt started to slap the top of the bedside table in an effort to find his phone. At last he had it, saw the caller display and groaned.

'Devlin,' he grunted. As he listened, he sat up and swung his legs to the ground. Finally, he spoke again. 'Has Preston been informed? Good. Tell him I'll see him there.' He disconnected the call as he stood.

Esme turned over. 'Was that the station?'

'Yes. I've got to go out. Go back to sleep, it's late.'

'Another case? Haven't you got enough on your plate at the moment?'

'Umm.' Matt donned his clothes as quickly as he could.

'Matt?'

'Look, I'm sorry, love. But I really have to get a move on.'

Something in his voice alerted her. She sat up. 'Is it connected with Blue Moon?'

'I can't talk now, Esme. And what about "go back to sleep" didn't you understand?' He was nearly ready to go.

'It is. Matt, what is it?'

He picked up his keys. 'I'm off. I'll see you later.'

At this time of night it could not be good. She sprung out of bed and pattered after him. 'Has someone else died?'

'Esme!'

'Has someone else been killed? Who is it? Matt, I need to know. You can't leave me in suspense.'

He turned at the door. 'It's late. Get some more sleep. I have very little information at the moment and if I don't get going I won't learn any more.'

'I won't be able to sleep. It's ridiculous to think I could.'

He hesitated. 'Okay. Someone has been found dead at Blue Moon. Rick and I need to get there as soon as we can. I'll let you have more details later, I promise.' He opened the door.

'Just tell me who it is, please, Matt.'

He slipped through the door, turned to close it and saw

her face. 'It's Lucy Strong – but, Esme, that has not yet been confirmed.' He shut the door and jogged over to his car.

Esme stood in shock. Lucy? Who on earth would want to kill her? And why? She stamped her foot. There was no chance of her getting any more sleep that night. She mooched into the kitchen to make a pot of tea. It was several hours before she could reasonably call Blue Moon. She wondered if she might go over there. Of course, it would have to be much later, when she could be assured Matt would have left. She prepared the pot of tea and extracted a mug from the cupboard before sitting down. Lucy? She could not credit it.

CHAPTER SIXTEEN

On their arrival at Blue Moon, Matt and Rick confirmed the dead person was Lucy Strong. They were taken to her room by Neil.

'Nothing's been touched, other than Sonja checking the poor woman was beyond help before she called the emergency services.'

'Good.' Matt walked in and looked down at the calm features. Surveying the room he saw her dressing gown tossed over the foot of the bed; the window and the door to the bathroom were both open. The light was on in the bathroom.

'Who switched the bathroom light on?'

Neil answered, 'It would have been Lucy. She invariably had it on all night, with the door slightly ajar.'

'Mmm.' Matt resumed his survey. The dressing table had the usual accoutrements of bottles, sprays and hairbrush and comb set. Her handbag lay on one corner. The wardrobe and dresser drawers were all closed. On the bedside table there was a lamp switched on.

'Who found her?'

'Celia Foster. It was a terrible shock for the poor woman. Sonja's with her now.'

Matt nodded as he mentally catalogued a mug, now empty of its original dark contents, a glass of water apparently untouched, a spectacle case and a book which, judging by its cover, was a lurid romance.

Having not touched anything, Matt exited the room just in time to see John Meadows approaching. Matt inwardly smiled as he noted how immaculately turned out the medical examiner was even at this hour. Meadows nodded a greeting at the three men as he passed. He was muttering something about the inconvenience of people dying suddenly in the middle of the night. The three left him to it and passed the duty SOCO team on their way downstairs.

Matt addressed Neil. 'We'll need to talk to Celia Foster.'

'I'm not sure that's possible. She really was in a state. I think Sonja took her to her room and sedated her.'

'In that case we would like to see Mrs Davies.'

Sonja entered the office where the two detectives waited.

'We won't keep you long,' Matt said. 'We'd just like you to take us through what happened tonight.'

Sonja clasped her hands in her lap as she gathered her thoughts. 'The first thing I knew, Celia was banging on my door, calling my name. When I opened the door she was verging on hysterics, but I did gather Lucy was dead. I told her to wait in my room while I went to check.'

Matt nodded.

'Lucy was, without doubt, dead, so I went back to my room and called the emergency services. I also called Neil. I tried comforting Celia but was not really making any headway. I was afraid she'd make herself ill. So I took her back to her room, gave her a sedative and stayed until she was asleep.'

'Ideally, we would have liked to talk with her tonight.'

'To be honest, I don't think it would have done you much good, Inspector. She was in deep shock and nearly incomprehensible.'

'Right. Well, thank you for your time. We won't keep you any longer for now.' Matt smiled. 'It's been a long night.'

'Yes.' She rose to her feet. 'I can't really believe she committed suicide, not Lucy.' She left the room.

Matt went back upstairs to find Meadows.

'Was it suicide? Or was she smothered?'

'I won't know the cause of death until she's been on my table.' He picked up the empty mug beside the bed and gestured to one of the team. 'I'll take this for analysis, as well.'

Matt's eyebrow lifted. 'Something in the drink maybe?'

Meadows did not answer.

'What about time of death?'

Meadows gave him a hard look.

'I know. Not until after your examination. But what's your best guess?'

'Within the last five hours.'

Matt sighed as Meadows told the ambulance crew they could now remove the body. As they walked together downstairs, Matt asked, 'Have you anything you can tell me?'

'No. Ideas, yes, but nothing concrete. As soon as I've finished my report I'll send it to you.' In the hall he paused. 'I'll put a rush on the post-mortem for you. That's all I can do at the moment.'

'Thanks, appreciate it.'

They parted company, Meadows going outside while Matt went to find his partner who was in the office with Neil.

'There's no more we can do here for now,' he said to Rick. Turning to Neil he went on. 'I'm sorry about this.'

Neil gave a weary smile. 'You'd think it would be easier the second time, but it isn't.'

'No, but there's no more you can do now either. Try to get some rest.'

'Right. I assume you'll be back later to see Celia?'

'Yes. We'll make it late morning, though. Give her a chance to be totally free of the sedative.'

As they went out of the front door, Matt said, 'It's around two-thirty now. Too late to go home and sleep. I think I'll go to the station, write up tonight's events and leave a message to bring the SIO up to speed.'

'Right you are. I'm going to try for at least a couple of hours' shut-eye. I'll see you later at the station.'

Matt nodded and walked across to his car. He turned as Rick softly called his name.

'Yeah?'

'I'm on to you, you know.'

'What are you talking about?'

'You don't want to go home and have to face Esme. I bet she's got a hundred questions for you!' He slipped into his car and quickly shut the door.

'Cheeky bastard.' But Matt was smiling as he got into his own car.

෨◌ඐ

In the end, after much thought, Esme decided to phone Sonja instead of going over to Blue Moon. At least then there was no risk of bumping into Matt, as he would not be best pleased. It was not that she wanted to upset him, but there was no way she could sit twiddling her thumbs until he came home and could keep his promise to let her know what was going on at Blue Moon.

She sniffed. Not that he would tell her much. More like the least amount he thought he could get away with. She poured the last cup of tea from the pot. She still could not get her head around the fact that someone had wanted to kill Lucy.

At ten Esme could not wait any longer. She rang Sonja's mobile.

'Hello, Esme. I suppose Matt told you of our tragedy?'

'Mmm. Terrible. It doesn't seem believable.'

'I know. Poor Celia found her. You can imagine the state she was in. In the end I had to give her a sedative. I don't think your Matt was best pleased as it meant he couldn't ask her any questions.'

'I'm sure he understood. Um, is he there now?'

'Not yet, but we are expecting him any moment.'

'You don't need to tell him I rang.'

Sonja laughed. 'Mum's the word.'

'How was Lucy killed? Was it like Rose?'

'I don't know. I only checked to make sure she was dead. She may not have been killed. There is some slightly guilty thought that she could have committed suicide.'

'Suicide? Lucy?'

'I know. It is difficult to believe.'

'Why would she? What reason could she have had? Did she leave a note?'

'I don't know is my answer to all of those questions. Maybe when Matt gets here, he'll have some answers. Although, I have to say, judging from past experience, he doesn't give away a lot.'

'No. That's Matt. Sometimes, it can be like squeezing water from a stone to get even the barest details.'

'Are you coming over today?'

'I don't think so. To be honest, I'd rather not run

into Matt. And I'd only be in everyone's way. I'll be over tomorrow as usual.'

'Okay. Possibly by then we'll have learnt a bit more about the situation.'

'How are Neil and Paula holding up?'

'Neil, surprisingly well. Paula thinks Selina returning home yesterday gave him a boost.'

'That was early. I thought the festival went on through the weekend.'

'It does. I gather there was a falling out with Zoggo. Scales dropped from Selina's eyes, break-up considered permanent.'

'I can certainly see why that would have bucked up Neil. Paula must be relieved.'

'She is, or was. I think Lucy's death has hit her really hard. It's now Neil trying to bolster her.'

'Sonja, I can come over, if you think it would help Paula.'

'No, don't worry. It'll do Neil good to look after her for once.'

'All right. I'll see you all tomorrow, then.'

࿊࿊࿊

At the police station Matt and Rick discussed the night's events.

'We're stuck until we know if it was murder or suicide.'

'Yes,' agreed Matt. 'It's difficult to know what type of questions to ask. As it is, we'll just have to keep them general.'

'If it is suicide, it might imply she killed Rose and the guilt caught up with her, I suppose.'

'The difficulty with that theory is when did she have the

opportunity? As far as I can see, she would have required complicity from one of the others, most likely Celia or Peter, or maybe both together.'

When they arrived at Blue Moon they found Sonja in the office.

'I know you have to speak with Celia, but she is still extremely upset and not yet over the shock of finding Lucy.'

'I appreciate that, but we do need to ask her a few questions. We'll be as easy on her as possible. We're not devoid of human kindness, you know.'

Sonja smiled briefly. 'I know that. Still, I wanted to ask if I could remain in the room? Sort of provide a bit of moral support for her.'

Matt exchanged looks with Rick, who shrugged. He looked back at Sonja. 'Very well, but only if you agree not to interrupt.'

'Thank you. Shall I go to fetch her now?'

'Please.' Matt sat behind the desk while Rick settled himself at the table Esme usually used. He made his preparations to record both electronically and physically what transpired.

Sonja returned, gently leading Celia. One glance was enough for both men to see how ravaged with grief Celia appeared. Sonja sat her facing Matt, saying quietly to her charge, 'I'll be here the whole time.'

Celia nodded and raised her eyes to Matt. 'I'm sorry. I was told you wanted to speak with me last night – or was it this morning?'

'That's all right, Miss Foster. We understand it's been a great shock.'

'We've been friends virtually all our lives.' Tears welled up in her red, puffy eyes. 'I just don't know how I'll get on without her.' She wiped her eyes with a sodden handkerchief. 'She didn't want to stay here after Rose. She was frightened, but I talked her out of it.' More tears cascaded as her voice rose. 'If only I could go back. I regret it so much now.'

Matt commiserated, 'Hindsight is always easy. Perhaps you can help us now in our investigation to find what exactly happened.'

'Yes.' She blew her nose. 'Of course.'

'Did she have any enemies, anyone she may have quarrelled with recently?'

'No. She's such a gentle soul.' More tears leaked out. 'Was such a gentle person, I should say.'

Matt adopted a firmer tone. 'Can you take us through last night? Everything you can remember.'

Celia inhaled and exhaled deeply before beginning. 'I was tired and went to bed early.'

'What time?'

'About nine, I think.'

'Right, go on.'

'I woke up with a peculiar feeling, a bit like nerves. Anyway, I couldn't drop off again. I kept going over and over our conversation at breakfast. I had suggested going out to the cinema and having a meal. Lucy refused. She was terrified we'd come back to another dead person. She was fixated on the killer striking again.' She drifted off in a brown study.

Matt called her attention back. 'Last night?'

Celia shook her head slightly. 'Yes, last night. The funny feeling wasn't abating and I couldn't help linking it with Lucy. Finally, I decided to check on her. The rest you know.'

'Was her door unlocked or did you have a key?'

'Lucy never locked her door, whether she was in there or not.'

'Odd, surely. If she was so concerned about a killer on the loose here, I'd have thought she'd have locked herself in.'

'No. Lucy had a problem with keys. She was forever losing them. For her, it was simpler to avoid them altogether.'

Matt raised a brow at Sonja, who nodded. 'When she first joined us, I think she mislaid four keys before she stopped using them.'

Matt redirected his attention to Celia. 'You went into her room…'

'I thought she was asleep at first. But as soon as I touched her, I knew something was very wrong. She was so cold. Still, I shook her a bit. I desperately wanted her to wake up and ask what I was doing. But she didn't. I can't remember clearly after that. I know I went to Sonja's room.'

'I see. When you were in Lucy's room, was anything out of place? Did you notice anything that could help us?'

'No. What kind of thing?'

'If it was suicide, generally a note is left. We couldn't find any such note.'

Celia appeared startled. 'Suicide? I thought she'd been killed, like Rose was.'

Matt soothed. 'Possibly. For now we haven't ruled anything out.'

'I see.' Celia's eyes dropped to her hands mangling the handkerchief in her lap.

'Why were you so sure she'd been killed? After all, you said there was no one here who'd wish her harm.'

She shrugged. 'I don't know. Maybe because she'd been talking about the killer being one of us, someone we knew. Maybe I thought the killer had struck again. Suicide, I don't think that had crossed my mind.'

'All right. I think we'll leave it there for now.' He took in her dejected stance. 'I'm very sorry for your loss.'

Celia nodded, stood up and subjected herself to being led away by the sympathetic Sonja.

Matt waited for the door to shut then said to his partner, 'As we're here, we might as well interview everyone else as a matter of form.'

The quick interviews revealed nothing helpful. Nobody seemed to have heard anything. However, Alice mentioned Wally's idea.

'He thought we should do some investigating ourselves.' Correctly interpreting Matt's expression as not one of wholehearted approval, she rushed on. 'It's not that we think you,' she included Rick with a quick glance, 'won't do all you can. It's just that Peter says he's one of your main suspects and Wally said being innocent wasn't always enough. That there have been miscarriages of justice before. You do understand, don't you?'

'Yes, I understand. Although I am, naturally, dismayed at your lack of faith and confidence in us.'

'Oh, I didn't mean that. Not exactly. It's just—'

Matt smiled at her. 'Don't worry. I do understand you're worried about your friend.'

'Yes, that's it.' Her soft voice conveyed her mortification.

'So, who's in this intrepid group of investigators?'

'Wally, Al and, of course, Peter.'

Matt closed the interview and, once alone with Rick, moaned, 'That's all we need.'

'I'd have thought you'd be used to it by now.' At Matt's puzzled look, he added, 'Esme.'

Matt had Peter brought back. He immediately enquired about the investigative group.

'Yes, that's right. We couldn't see any harm in it. And,

to be honest, it made me feel better – actually trying to do something myself. I'm well aware I'm one of your chief suspects.'

Matt decided to let that slide. 'Did your group turn up anything of interest?'

'No. Bit of a disappointment. But still, it's early days.'

'We would prefer you left the investigation to us.'

'So you want us to stop?'

'Ideally, yes. It could make things more difficult for us. Not to mention the danger to you and your friends if your questions should make the murderer nervous.'

Peter nodded. 'Right you are then.'

'However, if you just happen upon anything useful, we would be grateful if you passed it on to us.'

Soon after, Matt was talking with Wally. 'Did you question everyone here?'

'Not me, personally. But between us I'm pretty sure we covered everyone. Not that it did much good.'

'Nothing that could help our enquiries?'

'No. It's a pity, though, about Lucy.'

'Yes.'

'I just had a feeling she was holding something back.'

'What something?'

'I don't know, she held it back. I'd hoped to talk to her again today. Do you think it, whatever it was, is what got her killed?'

CHAPTER SEVENTEEN

The following morning Matt stared at the incident board, oblivious to the bustle and conversation going on throughout the open-plan office of the detective division. Rick took pains not to disrupt his partner's reverie, well aware of Matt's deductive processing.

Matt picked over in his mind all the scattered threads of information in front of him, as well as everything he could remember that Esme had told him about Blue Moon and its residents since she had begun to get involved with them. After a while he picked up a dry wipe pen and began to plot the various relationships on the board. Once finished, he stepped back to survey his handiwork. At last he began to see a vague sequence emerging. It still left questions, but fewer people remained in his corral of suspects. He glanced at his watch then spoke to Rick.

'How about we break for lunch now so we don't have to rush back for our meeting with the SIO?'

'Fine by me.' The two men grabbed their jackets. 'Did you get any breakthroughs this morning?'

'I've got some ideas but not a blinding flash of certainty. We can talk about it over lunch.'

Meanwhile at Blue Moon, Esme looked up from her computer as Paula, followed by Sonja, entered. Seeing their faces, she straightened. 'Everything okay?'

'Yes,' sighed Paula as she sank into the chair behind Neil's desk. 'It just feels all wrong.'

Sonja plugged in the kettle before turning and leaning against the table. 'Lucy's death seems to have hit everyone exceptionally hard. The atmosphere among all the guests is so… so muted.'

'Yes,' agreed Paula. 'Muted and heavy. The whole atmosphere is oppressive.'

An unhappy silence fell as the kettle boiled and the tea was made. As she handed a mug to Esme, Sonja said, 'With your new pact, I suppose Matt didn't tell you anything useful?'

Esme pulled a disgusted face. 'He promised when he left to come here that he would reveal all later. But all he said last night was that Lucy had died; cause of death not known yet; whether it was suicide or murder – not known yet. In other words, nothing I did not already know!'

Paula smiled in commiseration. 'Cheer up. Wally's group of investigators got warned off by your Matt.'

'Group of investigators?' Esme queried.

Paula explained, 'Yes, you know, carrying out their own investigation.'

Esme shook her head. 'I didn't know anything about that.'

Sonja carried on. 'Wally and Al, with Alice and Peter, decided the police didn't seem to be making any headway in finding the killer.'

'Matt must have loved that!' Esme interjected with startled amusement.

'Well, I don't suppose they put it to him quite like that. More likely they were tired of just sitting about and feeling useless, while the killer walked amongst them. Their biggest concern was that Peter was considered a prime suspect by the police and could end up being charged. They wanted to take some constructive action to prevent that happening.'

Esme smiled. 'Peter's got some good friends.'

Sonja nodded. 'Yes.'

'I wonder if that's where Matt's cryptic question came from this morning.'

'What cryptic question?'

'He asked if I knew anything about Rose's death which Lucy may have kept to herself. When I asked what he meant, he just said it was something someone had mentioned. Maybe one of Wally's gang picked up on it.'

Another contemplative silence fell as the three of them finished their tea.

❧❦

After lunch and back at the police station, Matt and Rick with Frank Shute gazed at the incident board.

'Starting with the basics,' Matt began. 'We have three distinct crimes: Rose being pushed down the stairs and her subsequent murder. Also, if it proves not to be suicide, the murder of Lucy Strong. The first question being: are we looking for three perpetrators or were they all done by one person?'

'Have we the pathology report?' Shute asked.

'Not the final formal one but I spoke with Meadows on my way back from lunch. He says the cause of death was a massive overdose of sedatives, traces of which were found in the mug that had contained her hot chocolate bedtime drink. No way to know if this was self-inflicted, that is, suicide or not. The mug only had Lucy's fingerprints on it, but that also is not conclusive as it could have been wiped clean before the drink was consumed.'

'What's your gut feeling?' Shute queried.

Matt thought a moment. 'I think she was murdered. Main reason being everyone seems to believe that Lucy was not the suicidal type. Added to which, Wally thinks she was holding information back concerning Rose's death. And the big question that follows: is this what got her killed? To ensure she did not pass on her knowledge?'

'Why does no one think she was suicidal? She could have been frightened about the killer, possibly someone she liked, being on the loose at the home. The strain could have proved too much for her.'

'It's true she did appear to have a nervous disposition. But, maybe as a result of that, she didn't hold her feelings in – a sort of safety valve. Also, worth remembering is that she left no note. Considering how close she was to Celia Foster, I'm pretty sure she would have left some message for her.'

'I see.'

'The only other reason she could have killed herself was guilt if she had killed Rose. The problem is, when could she have done it? She would have needed compliance at the very least from one of the others – most likely from Celia.'

'Perhaps that explains the lack of a note. Celia would have known why she'd done it.' Shute played devil's advocate.

'Mmm.'

'But you're not convinced?'

'No, sir.'

'All right. For now we'll go on the hypothesis that she was killed. So where do you go from here?'

'Well, if we start with the push down the stairs. Penny Childs says she heard a man arguing with Rose about the time we think she fell. So can we assume neither Alice, Sonja, Celia nor Paula could have done it, based on the fact they're women? Did the pusher return later to finish her off, or were these two actions done by different people?'

'If committed by the same person, with the women ruled out, it makes a strong case for Peter Francis being our culprit,' Shute pointed out.

Matt nodded. 'From early on, I've had the feeling that protectiveness is the key to all three crimes.'

Rick interposed. 'It certainly kept recurring. We were told Peter was protective of Alice, Celia of Lucy, Larry Dunns of Penny Child and, an outside chance, Sonja of the residents.'

Matt demurred. 'Not Sonja. Oh, I agree she's protective, but not to the extent of killing perceived threats. Plus, her protectiveness also covers the Carstairs and the effect murder would have on Blue Moon. Indeed, has had. On the business side it would be too high a price to pay.'

'So,' Shute sought clarification, 'who is left on our list of suspects?'

'I'm inclined to rule out Jane Masters, Penny Childs, Larry Dunns and Bob Pargeter based on they're all too absorbed in their own interests.'

Rick asked, 'Even Larry? No love lost between him and Rose.'

Matt conceded the point. 'All right, we'll keep him as a possible, though frankly I can't see a good motive. He had already dealt with Rose's threats.'

'What about Green?' asked Shute.

'Again, I can't see a real motive, other than general dislike of the woman.' Matt paused. 'Yet, I don't think we should completely rule him out. He's definitely holding something back.'

'So that leaves him, Peter and Celia in our pool of suspects.'

'Yes.'

Rick mused, 'It's interesting that both bodies were found by Celia Foster. Is that coincidence, bad luck or an avenue we should pursue further?'

'Something to bear in mind, anyway,' Shute said. 'Anything else?'

'Just that we need to work on finding answers to various questions,' Matt replied.

'Such as?'

'Why would Rose be coming downstairs at that time of night? Where was she heading? What was the murky incident in Rose's past that Larry used to neutralise her? Why was Peter Francis awake? Why did he go downstairs? Was it really simply that he was nosy? If it was him who pushed Rose, was he shocked to learn Rose was still alive? And, finally, what happened to the missing items from Rose's room: no money at all, no notebook, diary or journal, and none of the letters she had received since her arrival?'

'Right. Plenty to be going on with. Let me know the answers you find.'

'Yes, sir.'

Rick looked at his partner. 'Why do you think she was coming downstairs?'

'Of course, I can't say for sure, but it's possible she was aiming for the office.'

'The office?'

'Yes. We know she was a blackmailer. She needed information and where are all the details of the residents kept?'

'Yes, I see. During the day there would be too much of a risk of someone walking in on her.'

'Exactly. At night she could safely take her time.' Matt sat down and flipped open his notebook. 'I'm going to sort out the questions I need to ask to get to the bottom of this. Can you chase up the investigation into Rose's background?'

'Will do.'

CHAPTER EIGHTEEN

In the morning, Rick found the results of the investigation into Rose's background on his desk. As he finished reading it, he whistled. 'It would appear our Rose married late, aged forty-five.'

'Not exactly the stuff that blackmail is made of, though,' commented Matt.

'No. But for about ten years prior to that she seems to have made her living as an escort slash call girl. She probably would not have wanted that to be common knowledge among the residents and staff of Blue Moon. Don't you think?'

Penny Childs was waiting for the two policemen when they arrived. Matt had rung Blue Moon the previous afternoon, requesting that those they wished to interview held themselves available.

Once the pleasantries and preliminaries were out of the way, Matt asked her, 'First, just to confirm you heard someone arguing with Rose the night she died?'

'Yes, that's right. A man.'

'You're positive it was a man?'

'Absolutely positive. I could hear him quite clearly – hear his voice, that is. But I couldn't make out the actual words.'

'Nevertheless, you heard the voice and tone?'

'Yes.'

'When you first heard it, what was your first thought of who it could be? Your instinctive view.'

'I didn't know who it was.' She frowned in thought. 'No, all I can remember is thinking there's Rose arguing again. Then I put it out of my mind.'

Matt pushed the query in various forms but Penny never deviated from her original claim. Finally, he threw in the towel. 'Thank you, Mrs Childs, for your time.'

Penny stood, then hesitated. 'I'd tell you if I knew who it was, Inspector. But I can't in all fairness just select a name to give you when I really don't know who it was.'

Matt smiled. 'No, of course not. Although it's a pity you can't identify the man. It would have helped us no end.'

Peter Francis was the next resident to be ushered into the office. He was taken over and over his actions on the night of Rose's death, but without the officers learning anything new.

'Why were you awake so late – or early – in the morning?'

'No idea. Maybe noises disturbed me. I couldn't say.'

'When Miss Strong told you that Rose had been found dead, why did you go downstairs? It's not as if you could have helped her.'

Peter shrugged. 'Who knows? The facts are that I was wide awake and I suppose curiosity played a part. Prurient as that might seem.'

'Did you hear an argument involving Rose earlier in the evening?'

'No.'

Matt switched tactics. 'You're friendly with Alice Littleton?'

'Yes, but what's that got to do with anything?'

'How friendly?'

'Friendly. All right?'

'Friendly enough to want to protect her?'

'Protect her from what?'

'I understand that, in several ways, Mrs Littleton was on the sharp end of Rose's malignancy.'

'Yes, well, Rose was an altogether nasty piece of work.'

'So you stood by Mrs Littleton?'

'Of course. And, I might say, so did the others.'

Matt nodded. 'How far would you be prepared to go to defend Alice?'

Peter stared at him, then gave a mirthless smile. 'Not as far as murder – certainly not as retaliation of a few slights that no one, including the others, credited in any way.'

'Did you wonder if Rose had upset Alice who, subsequently, in a fit of anger may have pushed Rose down the stairs?'

'No. Categorically not. Alice would never react like that. It's not in her nature.'

Ignoring his words, Matt carried on with his theory. 'Then when you discovered Rose was not dead and you found yourself conveniently alone with her, did you decide to ensure she could cause no more hurt or distress to your friend?'

'No,' said very quietly.

As he watched the door close behind Peter, Matt sighed heavily. 'It's so irritating. He's the perfect suspect, but each time I interview him the more convinced I am of his non-involvement.'

Rick grunted his sympathy as he left to fetch Charles Green.

This interview did not go smoothly either. Frustrated at Green's obdurate refusal to tell them all he knew, Matt warned, 'Withholding information could be taken as obstruction of a police investigation, which is an offence.'

'I'm not withholding any information.' Green's raised voice testified to his loss of control. 'If I knew any facts, I'd tell you. But I can't and won't give you my suppositions. For God's sake,' he was close to shouting, 'it'd probably send you off in the wrong direction completely.' More quietly, he carried on, 'Not to mention it could make a probably innocent person suffer your interrogation techniques.'

Seeing no point in further questioning at this point, Matt let him go. The two detectives decided to break for lunch and took themselves off to the Dog and Duck for a beer and sandwich.

On their return to Blue Moon, they immediately saw Esme explode from the front door. Rick smirked. 'Your lady's obviously keen to speak with you.'

As Matt parked, Esme rushed over to his door before he had a chance to get out. 'Thank goodness. I thought you were never coming back. And why aren't you answering your phone?'

Matt stood up. 'What's the matter?' He eyed her warily. 'Is this about the case?'

'Of course it is.'

'What are you doing here, anyway? This isn't one of your Blue Moon days.'

'I'm trying to tell you, if you'd just be quiet and let me.'

Matt heard Rick snicker. With what dignity he could summon he ignored him and said to her, 'Go on then.'

'Right. I gather you talked with Penny this morning. You wanted her to identify the man she heard arguing with Rose.'

Matt nodded. He was not going to make the mistake of talking.

'Well, just before lunch she was outside and passing by the office window when suddenly she heard a man shouting. She says it is the same man she heard with Rose.'

Rick whistled. Matt said to Esme, 'She's positive?'

Esme nodded.

'Why didn't she come to us?'

'She tried to, but you'd gone. She couldn't find Sonja or Paula so, naturally, she called me.'

'Naturally!' He kissed her quickly. 'Now go back to whichever client you left in the lurch.'

'Who was it, then?'

'I thought Miss Childs told you.'

'She recognised the voice but couldn't say who it was.'

'I see.' He turned towards the building. 'I'll see you later, Esme.'

'Matt!'

'I'll tell you all I can tonight. Now I've got to get her confirmation and people to question.' He strode to the entrance. Rick wisely fell into step beside him.

'Was that quite fair?'

'Yes. We need to get confirmation about this man before rumours start to abound. Plus, I'm trying to dissuade Esme from interfering in police work.'

'Good luck with that!'

After checking the facts with Penny, Charles was recalled to the office. He did so reluctantly but the alternative of being taken to the police station persuaded him to comply.

Matt decided on the direct approach. 'Your voice has been identified as that heard arguing with Rose on the night of her death.'

'Identified? Who by?'

'That doesn't matter. The important point is it was recognised.'

Green looked doubtful. 'Why haven't you claimed this before?'

'Because I'm sure when you argued with Rose, your voice was raised. Just as it was this morning when it was overheard by the same person who heard the argument with Rose.'

There was an extended silence before Green sagged back in the chair. 'All right. I did have words with Rose. God, that woman would try an angel. I had no intention of physically harming her, or even touching her, for that matter. But she was such a malevolent creature. She was taking so much pleasure from the misery she was causing that I just lashed out.' He stared out of the window. 'It was spur of the moment. One minute she stood there sneering, the next she was crashing down the stairs.' He looked Matt in the eye. 'It just happened. It wasn't a planned attack or anything like that.'

'Did you go to check on her?'

'No. She was lying so still, I assumed she was dead. I just went to my room and hoped no one had seen me. Not my finest hour, I admit.' He sighed. 'You probably won't believe this, but when I found out the fall had not killed her, I was incredibly relieved.'

'You're wrong. I do believe you.'

CHAPTER NINETEEN

A car was called to collect and transport Charles to the station where his formal statement could be taken. In the office, Rick mused, 'I feel a bit sorry for him. I'm inclined to think it was as he claims. Rose, being her usual acrimonious self, causing him to lose control for one second.'

'Yes, I agree. Still it would have been better if he had owned up from the start.'

Rick grinned. 'If everyone did that there would no need for us!'

Matt gave a gust of laughter. 'There is that, of course.' He looked down at his notebook. 'Still, we've yet to find our killer.'

Rick was silent for a brief moment before querying why Penny had not earlier recognised his voice.

'It's possible because Charles is normally reclusive and softly spoken.'

'Yes, you are probably right,' agreed Rick. 'Anyway, back to finding our killer, I think it has got to be one of the three left alone with Rose and, as we've removed Sonja from our list of suspects, that just leaves Peter and Celia.'

'Mmm. I still think Peter is not the type to smother her. He'd be more physical – bash over the head, strangle type.'

Rick grimaced. 'Not a flattering view of his character.'

'No. But, on the other hand, I'm pretty sure he is not our killer.'

'So that leaves Celia.'

'Yes. She's pragmatic, but is she cool enough to take a cushion and hold it down on Rose, when at any second someone could find her doing it?'

The two sat in contemplative silence until Matt said, 'We've been going on the premise that the person who killed Rose also killed Lucy Strong. Celia is genuinely grief-stricken over her friend.'

'Yes.' A pause. 'Could there be two killers involved?'

Matt shrugged. 'God, I hope not.' After another pause, he continued, 'We'd better have her in.'

'I'll fetch her.' Rick stood up but paused as Matt continued speaking.

'I think we should take her to the station. Interview her in a more formal setting.'

So it was in the dying part of the afternoon that Matt and Rick faced Celia across the table in a police interview room.

'Are you sure you don't want a legal representative?' Matt again asked.

'Yes. Absolutely.'

'And do you feel physically up to being questioned now?'

'Yes. Of course, I'll always miss Lucy. She's been a part of my life almost as far back as I can remember. I feel as if a part of me is missing.' Tears leaked before rolling down her cheeks. She extracted a tissue from her sleeve, wiped her face then blew her nose. 'I just wish, oh God how I wish, I could have saved her.'

Matt started by going over questions asked earlier in the investigation concerning the night of Rose's death. Celia's answers tallied with her previous statements. Then Matt leaned back in his chair.

'As it looks as if Lucy may have taken her own life, the only motive we can see is guilt.'

'Guilt?'

'Yes. If she killed Rose, her feelings of guilt may have become too much for her.'

Celia stared at him. 'Of course she didn't kill Rose. Lucy couldn't.'

'It didn't need any particular strength to hold a cushion over Rose's head. She was unconscious. There would have been no struggle.'

Celia leaned forward and looked Matt hard in the eye. 'When I say she couldn't, I mean that it was not in her psyche to kill anyone. I wasn't referring to her physical capability.'

Matt glanced at Rick. 'We can see no other possible reason for her to take her own life.'

'It's ridiculous to even think it,' Celia quickly responded.

'We don't think so.'

'You didn't really know her. But when you talked to her, surely even you could see her basic nature. There's no way she did it.'

'I will admit there was one stumbling block in our reasoning.'

'And what was that?'

'According to all the evidence, she was never alone with Rose that night.'

'There you are then. Obviously she could not have done it.'

'However, it is possible someone else was there,

prepared to cover her back, so to speak.' A pause, then softly, 'Someone such as yourself, perhaps. A very close friend.'

She looked a bit shaken. 'No. That didn't happen.'

'How did it happen, then?'

A silent Celia stared at him. More tears trickled out. Then her shoulders slumped. She whispered into her already sodden tissue.'

'I'm sorry,' Matt said. 'What was that? You must speak up for the tape.'

Celia became momentarily defiant. 'I did it. I killed Rose.'

'You killed Rose?'

'Yes. That's what I said.'

'Tell us exactly what happened after you returned to Blue Moon from your night out.'

'We, Lucy and I, came in and found Rose lying at the bottom of the stairs. We thought she was dead. I sent Lucy to fetch Sonja, who quickly came down, checked Rose and said she was still alive. She then called Dr Saunders.'

'Yes?' Matt prompted as she appeared to have stalled.

'Then Lucy, with Peter in tow, arrived. I didn't want Lucy to be there, she's not good in such stressful situations, even though I told them that, in fact, Rose was not dead and the doctor was being fetched. Anyway, Peter suggested I take Lucy to her room, which I did before returning to the hall.'

'Why did you return?'

'I felt obligated. Sonja had asked me to stay while she made her call.'

Matt nodded. 'I see. Go on.'

'Sonja reappeared and Peter went back upstairs. Then she asked me to stay for longer with Rose while she put some clothes on and let Neil know what had happened.' She stopped talking.

After a pause, Matt prompted again, 'And then?'

'I looked at Rose and thought it couldn't have happened to a better person. Then I began to realise she would be taken to hospital, patched up and returned here. Everything would carry on as before. I remember thinking how it was a pity she hadn't been killed in the fall. Then I thought, why not? Just stop her breathing and things could go back to how they had been pre-Rose. Before I knew it, I'd done it.' She stopped and met Matt's eye. 'It wasn't premeditated, you know. It just seemed the right thing to do at the time.'

'And Lucy?'

'Lucy wasn't involved in any way and knew nothing about it.'

'So why did Lucy have to die?'

'I would have given anything for that not to happen.' Her voice became very quiet. 'It was at breakfast on Saturday. I saw something in her eyes – only briefly, but it shook me. How could she have even contemplated it for a second after all the years, decades, that we had been friends? Nothing would ever have been the same after that. It was a truth I noticed over the rest of that day and Sunday.' She exhaled wearily. 'I put the overdose in her bedtime chocolate drink. She wouldn't have known or felt anything.'

Matt glanced at Rick, who got to his feet. 'I'll get the statement ready for signing.'

As he left the room, Celia quietly said to Matt, 'I think I knew you'd ferret out the truth eventually. If I was arrested, Lucy wouldn't have managed without me. In a way it was a kindness.'

'She had friends at Blue Moon, I'm sure someone would

have taken her under their wing. Are you sure you didn't kill her in case she said something to us?'

Celia shrugged before seeming to lose herself in her own thoughts.

CHAPTER TWENTY

When Matt arrived home it was to find Esme positively vibrating with eagerness to learn what had happened. He was not cruel enough to make her wait too long.

'Turns out we were right almost from the start that protectiveness was the overriding motive. So,' he finished off, 'all is now sorted out bar the paperwork and trials.'

'When do you think they'll take place?'

'Difficult to say. Although, as both of them are entering a guilty plea, not as long as if a protracted trial of proving guilt was required.'

Esme was pensive. 'I can't help feeling sorry for them.'

'Esme, I appreciate you know and like them, but people have to pay the price if they break the law. Otherwise you'd be on the road to anarchy.'

'Oh, I know that. It's just neither of them are real criminals – well, Celia was, probably. She did kill.'

'Twice,' Matt put in pithily.

'Yes, all right. But Charles, he just reacted badly in a split second. And, he didn't actually kill Rose.'

'No, and all that will be taken into consideration. As well as the fact he didn't go down to check on Rose.'

Esme heaved a disconsolate sigh. 'Still, I can't help feeling if Rose had never blighted Blue Moon with her presence, none of this would have happened.'

Matt shrugged. He felt that was pretty self-evident.

'Matt, were all your missing items accounted for in the end?'

'Yes, I think so. The money, I assume, was taken by the nephew. The journal probably never existed, although I still think it odd she kept no record of her future commitments. As for the letters, it transpires Charles took them, as well as some papers, after Rose's fall, and destroyed them. I think his aim was to get rid of any muckraking she may have dug up.'

❧❧

The following morning at the station Matt and Rick received congratulations and jokes from their colleagues for a case tied up neatly. Frank Shute also summoned them to his office for a final briefing.

'I take it there are no loose ends that may trip us up later?'

'No, sir. Both have signed full confessions.'

'Good. Congratulations on a job well done. Just make sure the paperwork is all in order.'

'Sir.' Grinning, the two detectives returned to their desks. At moments like this, life was good.

Later on, at home, he found Esme full of news after her usual morning spent at Blue Moon.

'You'll never guess,' she carried on without giving him a chance to make any attempt to do so. 'But Peter said he felt so relieved that he was now off your suspect list, that it gave him the courage to tell Alice about his feelings and propose to her.'

'What was her answer?'

'She said yes, of course.' Esme thought a moment. 'I wonder if Larry will finally ask Penny to marry him now. Maybe with all this romance and weddings in the air, Sonja will at last give in and start going out with Dr Saunders. It would certainly be a change for a retirement home to have two, possibly three, weddings – or maybe a double or triple one!'

'You don't think you might be leaping ahead a bit?' Matt queried. She giggled. 'I gather not much work got done today with all this love and passion floating about?'

'That's where you'd be wrong, Matt, you're so cynical! But with the arrests in all the papers, prospective residents have been calling and Neil is in his element sorting them out. I have to say, Paula looks a different woman – what with Selina back on track and a return to a potential full house at Blue Moon, Neil's blood pressure has come right down.'

As Esme tripped off to check if their supper was ready, Matt tossed around in his mind the subject of marriage – his to Esme. But then he shook his head. No, she was not ready yet, still getting accustomed to co-habiting with him. He should be patient, for a while longer at least.

As they settled down to eat, Matt said, 'Lucy was killed because she was beginning to see what had happened with Rose.'

'Yes.'

'I just hope you learn a lesson from that.'

'Lesson?'

Exasperated, Matt waved his fork at her. 'Yes, little Miss Echo. When you poke your nose in matters that don't concern you, you might learn something that could get you killed.'

Esme laughed. 'You are a rat fink. Anyway, I'm not a meddler, I'm just interested in people and, if they have any problems, in those as well.'

'Be interested in people by all means, but please leave their problems alone. The worry is starting to turn my hair grey prematurely!' Matt said in a heartfelt tone.

Esme laid her hand over his. 'I'll still love you when you sport a white thatch!'

This book is printed on paper from sustainable sources managed under the Forest Stewardship Council (FSC) scheme.

It has been printed in the UK to reduce transportation miles and their impact upon the environment.

For every new title that The Book Guild publishes, we plant a tree to offset CO_2, partnering with the More Trees scheme.

For more about how The Book Guild offsets its environmental impact, see www.bookguild.co.uk